Also by Daphne Ashling Purpus

The Draconia Novels

Dragon Riders
The Egg That Wouldn't Hatch
Dragon Magic
The Dragon Who Chooses Twice
The Girl, the Gryphon, and the Dragon
The Mage's Dilemma
The Seer's Challenge
The Dragon and the Unicorn

The Dragonwind Novels

The Fox, the Stag, and the Dragon
Dragon Sanctuary
Dragons, Mages, and Magic
Dragons and Other Outliers
Dragons, Waifs, and Influencers
Dragons in Peril

DRAGONS IN PERIL

DRAGONS IN PERIL

by

DAPHNE ASHLING PURPUS

ISBN: 978-1-7326402-5-2

Purpus Publishing, Vashon, WA

Never underestimate the valuable and important difference you make in every life you touch. For the impact you make today has a powerful rippling effect on every tomorrow.

—Anonymous

If dominating and destructive relations to the earth are interrelated with gender, class, and racial domination, then a healed relation to the earth cannot come about simply through technological "fixes."
It demands a social reordering to bring about just and loving interrelationship between men and women, between races and nations, between groups presently stratified into social classes, manifest in great disparities of access to the means of life. In short, it demands that we must speak of eco-justice, and not simply of domination of the earth as though that happened unrelated to social domination.

—Rosemary Radford Ruether (1936–2022): American feminist scholar and Roman Catholic theologian known for her significant contributions to feminist theology and ecofeminist theology)

TABLE OF CONTENTS

LIST OF CHARACTERS AND PLACES

Agatha: An elderly blind lady who stands tall and straight, with white hair, blue eyes, and a very kind smile.

Aloysius: Estrea's most learned historian. He lives in the palace in the turret where the archives are stored.

Althea: Illyra's many times great-grandmother who was a dragon rider at the time when the humans turned on the dragons.

Bergamen: A small, nearly translucent, light purple dragon with one damaged wing.

Blossom: A pink female dragon who is the best healer among the dragons.

Chauncey: A large telepathic dog who has wolves in his ancestry. He is black, gray, and white. He and Illyra are telepathically bonded.

Criseda: A turquoise female dragon who serves as the dragon ambassador to humans and who works closely with Ty.

Dragonwind: Ty's village, which is near the dragons' Aerie.

Driselda: A large emerald-green dragon who is the historian for the Aerie.

Edward: The smallest fox in the fox communication network, now bonded to Fen.

Elfrida: A retired schoolteacher living in Dragonwind.

Ernest: The nearly four-year-old son of King Bertram and Queen Elicia.

Esme: A sixteen-year-old girl with magical gifts who was abused and tortured by her parents but now lives with Martha, who is her guardian. She is short and thin, with short brown hair and kind brown eyes.

Esther: Sage's lady's maid.

Estrea: The nation ruled by King Bertram, which contains the village of Dragonwind.

Felicity: The nanny for the youngest three of Elicia and Bertram's children.

Felix: An eight-year-old orphan who is being fostered by Naomi.

Fenry-Fenria (nickname Fen): A sixteen-year-old nonbinary youth who is extremely thin, with short, cropped blond hair and blue eyes, wearing androgynous clothing.

Fergus: A heavyset wealthy baron, the father of Illyra and husband of Sage.

Foster: A green male dragon.

Foxy: A black cat who lives with Ty.

Fryzal: A young female dragon of many colors who calls out to Illyra. They become a bonded pair.

Gundryd: A bright yellow dragon who is the same age as Fryzal and who chooses Raymond as his bonded partner.

Harmony: A sea-green dragon who is in charge of the nursery for the youngest dragons.

Harriet: A six-year-old twin daughter of King Bertram and Queen Elicia.

Hazel: A six-year-old twin daughter of King Bertram and Queen Elicia.

Henry: The steward at King Bertram's palace.

Humphrey: The leader of the capital merchant guild.

Illyra: The seventeen-year-old daughter of Baron Fergus and his wife, Sage. She is tall, with an average build and dark brown hair and eyes. She has a telepathic bond with her dog, Chauncey.

Jade: One of the dragons who was forced to live in the Aerie when humans betrayed the dragons who had helped them. Jade was bonded with Obadiah, Fen's distant ancestor.

Jasper: A sixteen-year-old boy with black hair, a dark complexion, and a wiry build, small for his age, with a lot of magical talent. His father is the former mage Rastan, and his mother disappeared when he was five.

Jeb: The gamekeeper and warden for the forests around Dragonwind. He and Ty are best friends. He is tall (taller than Ty) and has a medium build, dark brown hair, and brown eyes.

King Bertram: King of Estrea. He is thirty-eight and is tall and well built, with dark brown hair and brown eyes. He is married to Queen Elicia. They have three sons and two daughters.

Kyle: A former hermit who now lives with Martha. He is tall and solidly built, with hazel eyes, nearly white hair, and a bushy gray beard. He is in his late fifties.

Lance: The twelve-year-old son of King Bertram and Queen Elicia.

Leo: A member of the palace guard.

Lyra: A sixteen-year-old girl who is very tall and thin, with an androgynous build, green eyes, and short brown hair.

Malcolm: A baron who was working with Fergus and who was also a member of the council.

Martha: A short, heavyset woman in her late fifties, with gray hair and eyes and a kind, plump face. She raised Ty after his parents were killed, and now she's raising Esme.

Matthew: A nine-year-old orphan who is being fostered by Naomi.

Matilda: A young fox who is bonded to Lyra.

Miranda: Malcolm's wife and the mother of nine-year-old Molly.

Mittens: A gray tabby kitten with white paws, a white chest, and a stubby tail.

Molly: The nine-year-old daughter of Malcolm and Miranda.

Naomi: Paul's mother, also rescued from the mining villages and now living in Dragonwind.

Obadiah: Fen's very distant ancestor who was bonded to the dragon Jade when the dragons were forced to live in the Aerie.

Olivia: A fox living in the forest behind the palace who is the capital link in the fox telepathic network. She and King Bertram can reach each other telepathically, and she can reach Rupert in Dragonwind.

Oscar: A young orange male dragon with yellow wings.

Paul: A nearly nine-year-old boy who was rescued from the mining villages. He is telepathic and bonded to Wilhelmina.

Prince: A black-and-white kitten.

Priscilla: An eight-year-old orphan, tall and thin, with blond hair and blue eyes, who is being fostered by Agatha and Elfrida.

Queen Elicia: A tall, slender woman with red hair and blue eyes; she's thirty-four years old and married to King Bertram. They have three sons and two daughters.

Raymond: The eighteen-year-old son of King Bertram and Queen Elicia. He is the eldest and is Bertram's heir.

Ribendi: An ancient predecessor race of dragons from which the current dragons developed centuries ago.

Robert: A six-year-old orphan who is being fostered by Naomi.

Rocking Rocks: A new village near Dragonwind, built on the location of an old, ruined mining town.

Rupert: A red male fox now living in Dragonwind. He runs the fox telepathic network between King Bertram in the palace and Ty in Dragonwind. He is friends with Samantha and Esme.

Sage: Illyra's mother and Fergus's wife. She is also telepathically bonded to a raven named Star.

Samantha: A gray telepathic squirrel who's a friend of both Rupert and Esme.

Sapphire: A bluish-purple female dragon. She is the leader of all the dragons.

Simion: The captain of the palace guards.

Spruce: The dragon bonded to one of the first riders back in Althea's lifetime.

Star: A raven who has a telepathic bond with Sage. She is descended from ancient ravens who were companions of the Ribendi and then the dragons.

Stella: A blind seven-year-old orphan, small and thin, with brown hair and eyes, who is being fostered by Agatha and Elfrida. She is bonded to Mittens, who also provides her with sight.

Stephen: One of the palace guards.

Timothy: One of the merchants from the capital.

Tobias: A very ancient philosopher who studied the legends and stories of Estrea.

Ty: A twenty-year-old who governs Dragonwind and also serves as an ambassador for King Bertram when needed. He has both telepathic and healing powers. His parents were killed when he was six, by which time he knew he was truly a boy born into a girl's body. After he caught those who killed his parents and exposed the crimes of the king's half brother, the dragons granted him the body that he should have been born with.

Tyler: A pharmacist in the slum district.

Ventus: A large blue dragon who was mated with Windsong. Bergamen is their son.

Wilhelmina: A large moose who is the strongest telepath on the planet.

Wilson: A refugee from one of the small mining villages along with his wife, Selena, and eight-year-old son, Ralph. He is the lead carpenter in Dragonwind.

Windsong: A nearly white dragon, translucent in tone, with just a hint of purple. She and Ventus were the parents of Bergamen.

Zythrym: One of the barons on King Bertram's council who follows Fergus's plan.

CHAPTER 1

ESCAPE

Illyra hid in the hall closet outside her father's office with her dog, Chauncey. The closet wasn't large, and the two of them barely fit inside, but they could hear everything that was said in her father's office. It was a musty guest closet that was rarely used since her mother's accident. Tonight her father was meeting with his inner circle of barons. Illyra knew that her father and the other barons were trying to take over the country of Estrea and remove King Bertram.

Illyra knew that all these men were greedy and unscrupulous, and they hated the way King Bertram was putting a stop to their exorbitant rents and usurious money lending. The king had already cleaned up the worst slum in the capital, and that's what prompted the barons to try to take over.

As she and Chauncey listened, she wondered what they could do to stop this group. But suddenly she heard her father saying, "We need to enforce the ancient laws. These laws are still on the books, and they'd allow us to hunt dragons if they leave their Aerie. I know this because one of my ancestors helped to draw up the treaty when the dragons were banished to the Aerie. I hadn't seen the actual treaty, but thanks to Zythrym, we now have an actual copy. I've never bothered with it before now, but since that do-gooder of a king changed our entire society, and since he has brought in the help from

1

the dragons to do what he'd failed to do before, I think it's time to enforce the laws that are still valid."

What? said Illyra to Chauncey. The two of them were able to communicate telepathically using their magic.

Chauncey, a large black, white, and gray wolfhound, replied, *That's not good at all.*

The two of them listened carefully. They heard one of the other men saying, "That would be wonderful. It would be much easier to hunt them here in the capital. After all, two of them live in a cave behind the palace."

Another man said, "When should we hunt? I'm available this weekend. Sounds like great sport."

Illyra's father, a man named Fergus, said, "Great idea. Let's plan on it."

Illyra looked at Chauncey and spoke telepathically. *We need to get to the king and warn him.*

Chauncey nodded and said, *Definitely!*

The two of them kept listening, but soon the meeting came to an end, and the men agreed to meet in the forest behind the palace on Saturday at dawn.

The men left, and finally Illyra's father headed to his bedroom. Once he was gone, Illyra and Chauncey raced to Illyra's mother, Sage. Sage had a suite on the first floor, right off of a lovely walled garden. It was a beautiful suite, decorated in warm colors, generating a feeling of warmth and calm. It was the only part of this house that Sage was allowed to control. Fergus ruled the rest of the large mansion with an iron hand.

Illyra knocked on her mother's door, and then she and Chauncey entered. She went over to her mother, who was sitting in an overstuffed chair, and kissed her before sitting in a chair near her. Chauncey curled up between Sage and Illyra.

"You won't believe what Father is planning," said Illyra.

"Something horrible, I'm sure," said her mother.

"He says that he's discovered ancient laws that allow for the hunting of dragons," began Illyra.

"Unfortunately," said Sage, "he's correct. It's actually not that unusual for ancient laws that have fallen into disuse to be forgotten. They aren't repealed, but they're no longer enforced."

"Well, we have to warn King Bertram," said Illyra.

"You need to leave for the palace tonight," said Sage calmly, as if Illyra's news wasn't a surprise at all. "I've actually been expecting something like this for a while. Since you turned seventeen two months ago, you are legally an adult, so Fergus has no rights over you. It's time for you to leave, and Bertram will protect you."

"But I can't leave you," said Illyra. "You need me."

"We both know that I'll never walk again," began her mother. "Your father saw to that when he pushed me down the central staircase. Thanks to Star here," her mother continued, reaching out to stroke the chest of the raven sitting on the back of her chair, "he wasn't able to finish the job and kill me. He just ignores me now, but he is planning to try to marry you off to one of his rich friends.

"You are the one who's in danger, and you must leave now," said Sage. "And you are the only one who can give a firsthand account of what the barons are plotting."

Illyra hesitated, unwilling to leave her mother, but finally nodded.

Sage smiled and said, "I've been planning for this day. I have some very ancient manuscripts written at the time that humans turned on the dragons who'd been so kind and helpful to them, and I think these documents might aid Bertram. They include a copy of this treaty, a copy which has been handed down in our family for centuries. I knew Fergus was aware of the terms, but I didn't realize he had an actual copy. There are not many of those after all these years."

"Apparently someone named Zythrym gave it to him," said Illyra.

"Well, however he got an actual copy, this does make Fergus more dangerous," said Sage as she reached into a drawer in the table next to her and pulled out a small satchel. She handed it to Illyra as she said, "Now, you and Chauncey must go immediately. Use my garden door and the secret gate on the other side of the garden and then head east through the woods to the palace."

"It's dark now," said Illyra, "which helps. But we'll get to the palace quickly as it's only a mile away, and I don't think I want to wake the king."

"Why don't you go to Oscar and Foster's cave?" said Sage, referring to the two dragons who lived in a cave behind the palace and helped guard the King Bertram.

"That's a good idea, and I will tell the king about everything and give him these documents. But once I meet with King Bertram, I am going to make sure he sets up a way to free you," Illyra said firmly.

Sage gave a sad smile and said, "Just be sure you talk to Bertram and that you safeguard that satchel. That's what's important."

Illyra nodded, gave Sage a kiss on her cheek, and headed with Chauncey for the door leading out into the garden.

Once outside, Illyra moved down the path leading toward the hidden gate. It was very dark, but Illyra and Chauncey knew the garden well. Illyra said, *It may be dark, but our sense of smell will take us in the right direction. Everything is coming into bloom, and here we have lavender.* She pointed to her right. *That will be followed by other herbs, such as rosemary, thyme, and of course sage.*

I can follow the scents, said Chauncey. *And when we start to smell roses, we'll know we're near the gate.*

That's right, said Illyra, smiling.

The two of them moved quietly but quickly through the garden, and they were soon at the roses. They moved carefully behind the trellis, avoiding the thorns, and they found the hidden gate. Illyra opened it quickly, and the two of them stepped out into the forest beyond.

Chauncey led the way as the two of them moved along the path. They knew this forest very well, but they were also being cautious. The documents in the satchel were too important for them to risk being caught.

They had about one mile east to go to get to the palace and the cave behind it. It didn't take them long, and before midnight they were within sight of Oscar and Foster's cave. Illyra called out telepathically to the dragons.

Oscar, Foster, we need help. Sage sent me and Chauncey to escape from my father and to bring news to King Bertram.

They watched for a few minutes, and then they saw a bright orange drag-on step out of the cave entrance. Illyra and Chauncey hurried over to him as Illyra said, "Hi, Oscar. I'm so glad to see you."

"You two are out late," said Oscar. "Come on in, and we will discuss your news with Foster, Edward, and Fen."

The three of them entered the cave, and Illyra looked around. She loved it here. Foster and Oscar had made the cave look incredibly warm and wel-coming. They'd hung some tapestries on the walls, depicting the mountain Aerie where most of the dragons lived. There were lots of big brightly col-ored cushions for guests to sit on, and Illyra and Chauncey made themselves comfortable.

As they were getting settled, Foster, Fen, and zer bonded fox, Edward, came into the large open living area. Foster, a bright green dragon, settled himself next to his partner and said, "Hey, Fen, would you want to make some tea for Illyra?"

"Sure," said Fen, who was being fostered by Oscar and Foster. Fen was a sixteen-year-old nonbinary adolescent, and ze was the first ever youth to be fostered by dragons.

Fen walked over to the kitchen area and began preparing tea for Illyra as Oscar said, "So how can we help you? What's happened to bring you here so late? Are you OK?"

Foster put out a front leg onto Oscar as he said with a chuckle, "Try one question at a time, and give her a chance to answer."

Oscar looked a bit embarrassed, but he said, "Well, we haven't seen Illyra in several weeks, and all of a sudden she turns up at midnight tightly clutch-ing a satchel. I'm worried."

Foster nodded as Fen walked over with mugs of tea for Illyra and zem-self. "Oscar's got a point," ze said as ze handed Illyra a mug and then took a seat next to Foster as Edward jumped up into Fen's lap.

Illyra looked at the four of them staring at her and finally said, "Chauncey and I fled at my mother's insistence. We didn't want to leave her, because she'll be in danger once my father discovers what I've done and what she's given me. We're going to have to rescue her as soon as possible."

"So, what's changed?" asked Foster.

"You are all in danger," began Illyra, "and I need to see King Bertram to tell him what my father and his barons are plotting. All of Estrea is actually in danger. My mother insisted that I bring this information to the king, but I didn't want to leave her. We have to rescue her."

Oscar looked as if he wanted to pull Illyra into a hug, although he no doubt realized that being hugged by a dragon wasn't necessarily the most comforting thing. Instead, he said in the calmest voice he had, "We will get you to the palace to meet with King Bertram first thing in the morning, and, of course, we will do our best to keep Sage safe."

Illyra said, "Thank you. Thank you, all of you," and she began to drink her tea.

As she did so, Foster said, "We have opened up a new portion of our cave as a guest room, now that Fen is living with us."

"Yes," said Oscar, "since we wanted to be sure Fen could entertain friends if ze so desired. We'd be happy to have you and Chauncey stay there tonight."

Foster added, "You do need to get some sleep, or at least rest. I know you're worried about your mom, but you'll want to be at your best when you explain everything that has happened to the king."

"I guess," said Illyra. "Thanks."

They all stood, and Foster guided Illyra and Chauncey to a hallway that led away from the main great room. "It's just down here," said Foster as they walked down the passageway. "Our room is here," he said, pointing over to a giant room with lots of cushions and pillows in bright colors, mostly orange and green.

Then they passed a second room, done in blues and purples, with a ledge covered in pillows and blankets. Along one wall there was also a small desk and dresser, as Foster said, "And this is Edward and Fen's room."

He then turned right into a passageway that looked newer, and Foster said, "We built the guest room right down here," as he stopped in front of what looked to be a more recent excavation.

"Wow," said Illyra as she took in a small cave-like room that was outfitted much as Fen's was, with a ledge covered in pillows and a duvet, a dresser over in one corner, and a small desk, along with a small dresser, in the other. "This is really nice!"

Chauncey said telepathically to everyone, *It sure is, and I see that you have a large bed on the floor that I can use.*

Foster chuckled before he said, "Yes, we haven't had a lot of guests, but most of Fen's friends have bonded animals. Fen has Edward, as you know, Esme has Rupert the fox and Samantha the squirrel, Lyra has Matilda the fox, Jasper has a dragon named Bergamen, and so forth. If you don't know all of them, you soon will."

"And thanks to my father, they are all in danger," said Illyra, frowning and looking worried.

Foster patted her and said, "Now, now. We will sort all this out, but not tonight. You need to turn off your worries and just get a good night's sleep."

"I'll try," said Illyra.

"I'll leave you to rest," said Foster, "but you know where our room is if you need anything."

"Thanks again," said Illyra.

Once Foster had left the guest room, Illyra took off her shoes and climbed onto the bed. When she was settled, she patted the spot next to her, and Chauncey jumped up. "Good thing that Foster and Oscar made this bed bigger than usual," she said as she hugged Chauncey.

I'll never leave you alone; you know that, Chauncey said.

I do, and I'm so glad to have you as my best friend. Let's see if we can take Foster's advice and get some sleep.

Illyra closed her eyes and, surprisingly, fell quickly to sleep. She started dreaming, and all of a sudden, she was seeing Estrea back in the time of the original dragon riders. One of the riders seemed to be speaking directly to her.

"Illyra," said the woman. "It's time we got to know each other. I'm your several times great-grandmother, and my name is Althea."

Illyra's mouth dropped open, and finally she said, "You know me?"

"Yes," said Althea. "I have helped Sage for many years, but I had to wait for the right time to contact you since you needed to be an adult and out from under your father's control. You have now accomplished both of those goals. Well done."

"So you know what my father is going to do?" asked Illyra.

7

"I know what he thinks he can do," corrected Althea. "However, he is not going to succeed. You and others will stop him. You absolutely must for the sake of both Estrea and, indeed, the entire planet. I'm going to help you by coaching you in the early history of dragons. I lived three centuries ago when humans first turned on the dragons. You will also need the help of Aloysius, the historian who lives in the palace, and the writings of Tobias, a historian and philosopher who was alive during my lifetime. Now, let's get started. What do you know so far?"

Illyra thought for a few minutes, trying to remember all that her mother had secretly taught her. Then she said, "At least five centuries ago, there was an ancient race of beings who came to this planet and who were called the Ribendi. They arrived when human life on this planet was very primitive, and they helped humans to learn better ways. Over time, the Ribendi evolved into what we now know as dragons. The dragons continued helping humans to develop a more advanced civilization, one that used tools to craft many new instruments out of metal and to build stronger homes, helping them settle into larger cities and to develop ways to govern themselves."

"All true," said Althea. "They also taught humans about healing plants, how to cultivate herbs and vegetables, and many other things. Things went well for about two hundred years, and a close relationship developed between the newly evolved dragons and humans."

Illyra said, "Until the humans turned on the dragons."

"Quite so," said Althea. "As the humans developed villages and cities, strife grew as a class society formed. The dragons always fostered cooperative societies, and, indeed, I now believe that it was the Ribendi who began that process. We can't know for sure, but I believe the Ribendi stayed because they believed that Estrea was a place where a truly nonviolent, supportive society could be fostered.

"However, as the population grew, so did the divisions. Men like the barons you know became more numerous, men who cared nothing for the well-being of others but only their own power. Fergus comes from that lineage, and you can see that he still follows that greedy and destructive philosophy.

"As they gained power, they also formed allegiances with others who hoped for the same kind of power. Once there were enough of them with influence and wealth, they realized that to fulfill their dreams, they needed to get rid of the dragons, who'd been trying to promote a more egalitarian society. They turned on the dragons, saying that dragons were just animals, fit for nothing but food, with no intelligence of their own."

At this, Chauncey, who had been monitoring Illyra's dream, said, *Humans are so arrogant. They think they are the only intelligent beings on the planet. That is so false.*

Althea chuckled and said, "You're right, Chauncey. And the dragons should have stood up to them then. It wasn't even all the humans. There were many who truly loved the dragons and appreciated all that the dragons had done for humankind."

"Then why did the dragons abandon their plans?" asked Illyra.

"They were both shocked and, more importantly, deeply wounded by the change in the human leadership. They didn't want to be anywhere they weren't wanted. So when the humans said that they could have the land that you know as the Aerie, the dragons all exiled themselves to that horrible, rocky piece of land, a place no humans wanted anyway.

"You haven't had a chance to see what it is now, but as you might imagine, they have turned it into a self-sustained community. They grow their own food, and they take nothing from the humans. Also, many of those humans who disagreed with the decision to turn on the dragons went into exile as well, and that's when things got more interesting."

"How so?" asked Illyra.

"This world had no magic when the Ribendi arrived," said Althea. "There was still no magic as the Ribendi evolved into dragons. But once the dragons were banished, and once this group of humans decided to go into exile with them, well, a synergy developed between the dragons and those humans. First, the dragons and humans formed bonded pairs, such as what you have with Chauncey."

"Cool," said Illyra.

Althea said, "It was. And over several generations, these bonded pairs developed what you call magic. All bonded pairs are telepathic, primarily because while dragons can speak in the human tongue, many other species, such as dogs, can't," she said, bowing to Chauncey, "and telepathy works with all species.

"Over time more gifts developed, and our connection is now one of your magical gifts, one that hasn't been present on the planet since my time. I think that's enough for now, but know that I'm going to help you. Now sleep soundly, my dear, sweet great-granddaughter. Take comfort from the fact that I do still have influence in this world, and I will be looking after both you and your mother."

With that, Illyra's dream ended, but she didn't awaken. Instead, she slept deeply and well.

CHAPTER 2

MEETING WITH KING BERTRAM

In the morning Oscar let Illyra and Chauncey know that King Bertram would see them all right after breakfast.

"Sounds good," said Illyra as Oscar put a big bowl of porridge in front of her. She noticed that he also had a bowl of dog food for Chauncey.

Seeing Illyra's look of surprise, Oscar smiled and said, "We have a wide variety of guests, so we keep different types of food in our pantry. Foster's motto is 'Be Prepared,' so we are."

Foster came into the eating area and chuckled. "Well, my system has never let us down."

Fen came in, followed by Edward, and sat at the table in front of zer own bowl of porridge, saying "Very true," as Edward ate his food out of a bowl next to Fen's chair.

Once everyone finished eating, the group left the cave and walked down a path leading through the woods toward the palace. When they reached the small, gated entrance, Foster told the guard on duty that they had an appointment with the king. The guard nodded and opened the gate.

They entered the grounds behind the palace, and Illyra noticed a lovely garden surrounding a large lawn area scattered with various toys. She remembered that the king and queen had five children, some of them still quite small.

The group entered through the back entrance into a large family room. Queen Elicia, a tall, slender woman with red hair and blue eyes, looked up from the floor where she was playing with Ernest, her nearly four-year-old son, and her twin six-year-old daughters, Harriet and Hazel. She smiled and said, "Welcome. And good to see you again, Illyra! How is your mother?"

"Doing well, I hope," said Illyra. "I hated to leave her, but she insisted."

"I know you come with disturbing news, so I won't keep you. Bertram is in his study. Just follow Oscar, Foster, Edward, and Fen, and you'll be able to let Bertram know all about it."

"Thank you, your majesty," said Illyra.

"No need for such formalities," said Elicia. "Your mother and I have been friends since before you were born."

Illyra nodded, and she and Chauncey followed the others to Bertram's study. Oscar knocked on the door, and when the king called out for them to come in, the six of them entered. Illyra had forgotten how big the study was, but it made sense when she knew he had a number of dragons as potential guests. Even though the room was very large, it still felt warm and cozy, with heavy drapes on the windows, a number of large comfy chairs in front of the king's large desk, an area rug on the floor, and two walls covered with book-cases filled to overflowing.

King Bertram stood as they entered and said, "Welcome. Good to see you, Illyra, although I understand you bring troubling news. I asked Ty and Criseda to be here as well."

Illyra saw Ty, a tall, slim twenty-year-old young man, sitting in one of the large chairs, next to which was a gorgeous turquoise dragon curled on the rug. Ty smiled and said, "We're here to help you."

Illyra nodded, clutching her satchel. King Bertram said, "Make your-selves comfortable, and we'll get started."

Fen and Illyra took chairs near Ty, Chauncey curled up under Illyra's chair, Edward did the same under Fen's, and Oscar and Foster found spots on the rug.

Once everyone was comfortable, King Bertram nodded to Illyra and said, "Why don't you explain why you are here?"

Illyra took a deep breath and then began, "My mother made me come to share what we've learned, but she's in danger from my father and needs to be rescued as soon as possible."

Bertram looked at Ty and then said, "We're aware of the situation with your father, and we will protect your mother, I promise."

Illyra opened her satchel and pulled out a thick sheaf of papers and placed them carefully on the king's desk before saying, "My mother insisted that I bring these to you. She's had them for years, and I believe they've been handed down from my many times great-grandmother, Althea, who as you may know was one of the original dragon riders."

King Bertram nodded, and Illyra continued. "My father has been gathering a group of like-minded barons who are very unhappy with the way you have improved the lot of the poor. The rebuilding of the former slum area," and here she smiled at Fen, who grew up there when it was at its worst and whose mother was killed in a slum explosion, orphaning zem, "has seriously cut into their income."

"Aw, how sad," said Fen sarcastically, who had developed a dry humor as ze matured.

"I agree," said Illyra. "I wondered what these men were up to, so I found a closet right next to my father's office where I could listen in to their meetings. They are actually plotting to bring down the government and restore the old order."

King Bertram nodded and said, "I knew they were unhappy, but truly everyone else is doing really well—not only the poor, but everyone else except for a few very wealthy barons. You know, I'm sure that your father is continuing to build substandard housing on the south side of the capital and to force his workers to borrow money from him at exorbitant rates. In essence, they are nothing but slaves. And the other barons are doing the same thing."

Illyra nodded and continued. "I know, and that's why I've been eavesdropping on my father's meetings. He's leading this group. But last night I heard something that chilled me to the bone. Apparently there is an ancient law that is still on the books that allows for the hunting of any dragons who are found outside the Aerie."

"What?" exclaimed Ty.

Illyra looked grim. "I didn't believe it, but my mother said it was true." Illyra pointed to the stack of documents and said, "My mother has kept copies of the laws for years, and her ancestors before her, because apparently they knew that this would happen again someday."

"That's horrible," said Fen, looking at zer foster parents.

"Yes," nodded Illyra. "They plan to start hunting this weekend, and it's already Wednesday morning. That's why my mother sent me to you last night. I know she's going to try to keep my father from learning about my disappearance, and I am legally an adult, but if he learns that I've come here with information about what's he's doing, he'll take it out on my mother.

"He's always suspected that she knows a great deal more about dragons than she's ever let on, and that she's passed that knowledge on to me. That's why he tried to kill her when he threw her down our marble front stairs, where she broke her spine. He was only stopped when Star, her bonded raven, raised the alarm and summoned help for my mother."

"Yes," said Bertram. "Alicia and I talked to her after that and tried to get her to seek sanctuary for you and her here in the palace. She refused. She said that you both needed to stay where you were until, as she put it, 'the time was right.' I guess she now deems that time to have arrived, both because you are now legally an adult, so he has no claim on you, and because of the direction his plans have taken."

"We have to get her out of there," said Illyra, panic rising in her voice.

"I agree," said Bertram, "and it needs to happen today, before your father learns that you are here. What is his schedule like?"

"He leaves after breakfast for his office at his construction company, and he usually stays until late afternoon," said Illyra.

Bertram looked at Ty and said, "Can you and Criseda get her?"

"We should be able to," said Ty. Then he turned to Illyra and said, "Do you have any ideas about the best way?"

"My mother loves to spend most of the day outside in her garden at the back of the house," said Illyra. "If you could land in the garden, you could get her and be out of there before anyone notices. To be honest, I've always suspected that her lady's maid, Esther, is a spy for my father, but my mother needs her assistance. However, my mother doesn't like anyone with her when she's in the garden, so that should help. And Star will defend her to the best of her considerable abilities."

Ty and Criseda both stood, and Ty looked at Bertram, saying, "With your permission, sire, we'll leave right now."

King Bertram nodded, and Ty and Criseda left quickly. Bertram then turned to the documents and said, "Do you know what else is in here?"

Illyra shook her head, then paused before going on. Finally she said, "I just found out something last night as I slept."

Everyone looked at her in surprise, and Fen said, "In your sleep?"

Illyra nodded before going on. "I've always known about magic, or at least it feels that way. When I was three or so, I told my mother that I could hear the cook's cat talking in my head."

The group chuckled at this, and Illyra smiled and continued. "My mother explained about telepathy, at least as well as she could to a three-year-old. She also told me that I must always keep my gift, which is what she called it, an absolute secret. And above all, I was not ever to let my father know.

"Since then, she's taught me a lot about telepathy, how to speak only to her, block others, and so forth. Just before my father attempted to murder her, she bonded with Star. At that time, she also found me Chauncey."

Illyra rubbed Chauncey's head for a few moments before continuing. "The last few years, I've suspected that my mother had more magical talents. She had explained that everyone who had magic was related to the first bonded dragon riders and that anyone with magic was at least telepathic, but that there were also other gifts that showed up when they were needed."

"That's true," said the king. "I have very limited telepathic abilities, and that's it, but for instance, Fen here has influencer magic. Ze can use it to convince people of a good course of action. Those with extra gifts are tasked with only using them for good."

For a moment Illyra seemed lost in thought as she pondered how to introduce the next point, which she knew would come as a shock to some present.

"Yes, that's what my mother told me," said Illyra. "That brings me to last night. I had just fallen asleep in Oscar and Foster's lovely guest room when my several times great-grandmother Althea spoke to me in my dream."

"What?" said Oscar.

"I've never heard of dream speak," said Foster.

"How cool is that?" said Fen.

"Yeah," agreed Illyra, smiling. "It was pretty cool. She explained that she couldn't enter my dreams until I was of age, and I just turned seventeen. She told me that she dream spoke with my mother and had done so for her mother and so on, back to when she was actually alive. She wanted to be sure that her descendants knew all about the documents she passed down to them and that they kept them both safe and secret.

"She asked me what I knew about dragons, and she seemed pleased that I knew all about the Ribendi and the evolution to the current dragons, and also how much the dragons had done for humankind and how hurt they were when humans turned on them.That's all she told me last night except that now the documents my mother's family had protected were needed and that she also would watch over my mother and me," concluded Illyra.

"What a beautiful gift you have been given," said Bertram.

Illyra kept her hand on Chauncey as she said, "Chauncey was able to participate as well, and he also talked with Althea and she with him."

Edward said, *Totally wonderful. Do you have any ancestors talking to you, Fen?*

They all chuckled as Fen rubbed Edward's head and then said, "No, sorry."

King Bertram brought the focus back to Illyra as he said, "Did she give you any further information?"

"No," said Illyra. "She just said that she'd known this day would come eventually. We know that for many years Sapphire kept the dragons isolated in the Aerie, only coming out when humans were hurting other species. But, as you all know, when Bergamen was born and bonded with Jasper, things changed. The dragons now are a stabilizing force in our society, helping when they can. Not all of them live in the Aerie. And they were an enormous help in rebuilding the slum area, which of course was a major blow to the corrupt landlords."

Fen said, "Sure were, and I'll never forget how the dragons danced to collapse all the tunnels under the slum area. It was an amazingly effective way to destroy the slum and get it ready to be rebuilt. All the previous efforts to clean up the slums hadn't worked."

Oscar said, "That was so fun! We were so glad to be able to do something so effective and just plain fun!"

Everyone chuckled at the memory before Illyra continued. "Well, the barons didn't find it very amusing, and now they're trying to bring down the entire society and depose you, sire. They are power-hungry, greedy, selfish men."

Just then Oscar looked at Foster and then said, "Ty's on his way back with your mother. He should be here in about fifteen minutes."

Illyra let out a big cry of relief. Then she looked at the king and said, "Thank you, sire, so much!"

King Bertram said, "I'll ring for morning tea, and let's take it with Elicia in the family room. Once we get your mother settled, which Elicia will be happy to do, we'll return here to plan for the assault on Saturday."

Illyra nodded as she thought back over all they had discussed. It was a lot to process, everything from escaping from her father's house to dream walking with Althea, learning about Dragonwind's history, and now meeting so many new beings. Her life was certainly changing. She wondered how the others were feeling about all of this.

CHAPTER 3

SAGE'S STORY

The group headed for the family room, and as soon as they walked through the door, Illyra saw her mother. She raced over to her and gave her a big hug. "I'm so glad to see you here, safe and well." Then she looked at Ty and Criseda and said, "Thank you both so much!"

King Bertram came over to Sage and said, "You are most welcome to stay with us for just as long as you want."

"Thank you, Bertram," said Sage, "and thank you, Elicia. You both are so kind."

Just then a maid brought in a tea cart, and Elicia said, "Let's all have some tea and snacks, and then Ty and Criseda can fill us all in on their rescue."

Felicity, the nanny, said, "If it's all right, I'll take Ernest, Hazel, and Harriet up to the nursery for their tea."

Elicia nodded and said, "Yes, that's a good idea. Thanks, Felicity. Lance and Raymond, you'll want to join us."

Twelve-year-old Lance and eighteen-year-old Raymond, Bertram and Elicia's two eldest children, nodded, and Raymond, who was an adult and Bertram's heir, said, "Thanks."

As Felicity was herding the three small children out of the room with promises of tea and cake in the nursery, two more teens came into the room along with their bonded partners. Ty looked over at the new additions and said, "Before I begin, let's be sure that everyone knows everyone. Welcome, Esme, Rupert, Samantha, Jasper, and Bergamen. I'd like you to meet Sage; her raven, Star; Illyra; and Chauncey."

Once everyone had been introduced, filled their plates, grabbed mugs of tea, and found comfy spots to sit in the well-appointed family room, with many comfy chairs, couches, and large floor pillows that were quickly taken by the four dragons—who were very adept at coiling their nearly fifteen-foot bodies into much smaller spaces than seemed possible—Ty began his story.

"Criseda and I did just as you suggested, Illyra, and landed in the garden where Sage was pruning roses. Thankfully, Sage had expected us, and she was ready to leave right away, with a small bag already packed. And that turned out to be a good thing, because no sooner did I have Sage settled onto Criseda's back, with Star on her shoulder, than Esther, her lady's maid, ran out from Sage's quarters, yelling, 'Stop. Leave her alone.'"

Ty continued, "Needless to say, I did no such thing. I grabbed Sage's bag and vaulted onto Criseda, and we took off immediately. Esther shouted after us, saying, 'The master will hear about this,' but we really didn't care."

Sage said, "Esther has been spying for Fergus for years. I've tried to get my own choice of lady's maid, but he never allowed that."

Elicia said, "Well, now you can have whomever you want to help you as you need."

Sage smiled and said, "Thanks, Elicia. You've been a good friend to both Illyra and me for years." Then after a pause, she continued. "Bertram, did you get all the papers I sent?"

Bertram said, "Yes, but I haven't yet had a chance to look at them. Illyra told us what her father was planning for this weekend, but that's as far as we've gotten."

"I understand," said Sage, "and I haven't shared this part with Illyra either. We're going to need Aloysius's help as court historian, and probably Driselda's as well since she's the historian for the dragons. However, let me get things started with what I know, knowledge gained from my several times great-grandmother, Althea."

"I've also told King Bertram and those in our meeting this morning about Althea. She came to me for the first time in a dream last night," said Illyra.

Those who hadn't heard the story looked puzzled, but Sage smiled at her daughter. "I'm so glad," she said. "I've wanted to share this gift with you for a number of years, but Althea said it couldn't be until you were both of age as an adult and away from Fergus.

"For those of you who haven't heard about this magical gift, the women in my family have the gift of dream travel. Althea has been dead for many years, of course, since she lived in the time of the dragon banishment as well as the first dragon bondings. Aloysius will be excited because we have a first-hand account of that time period, and we also have the ability to ask Althea questions."

I talked with her as well, said Chauncey proudly, and all the others who were telepathic looked at him in wonder.

Sage smiled and continued. "The documents that Illyra brought you, Bertram, have been kept secretly in my family since Althea's time, since we knew they would one day be needed. That time has unfortunately arrived."

"Illyra said something about a law that is still on the books that permits the hunting of dragons," said Bertram.

Sage waited for a number of cries of dismay to dissipate before she began to describe the breakdown of dragon-human relations to the group. She told them of the change in the dragon-human interactions once the humans had stopped being a nomadic people and began to live in larger groups, forming cities and towns.

Sage described how as they developed a more advanced civilization, they also developed strict social hierarchies. When dragons tried to show them the drawbacks to such an unequal arrangement, those in power quickly decided that the dragons were no longer needed and, in fact, were harming their plans.

These power-hungry humans turned on the dragons and began calling them stupid animals and worse, even though dragons had really helped establish human civilization here in Estrea. Sage continued by telling how this change in dragon-human interactions deeply wounded the dragons, who had only wanted to make life for every species better. The dragons gave up the struggle and agreed to take a horrible piece of land that no one else wanted and to stay out of human life.

Sage concluded by saying, "The humans drew up the treaty and put in the clause that any dragons found outside the Aerie's boundaries could be hunted and killed. One of Fergus's ancestors helped draft this treaty, and Fergus has gloated about it in the past. But he never had a copy of the treaty or needed to try to get it enforced until you, Bertram, used the dragons to help clear the slums and destroy the power of Fergus and the other barons. After all, before that, the dragons didn't care about or interfere with human society, with very few exceptions. They just withdrew from the world, along with the handful of humans who did love and appreciate them.

"They were able to rework the land, and over time, they've made the Aerie into something that gives them total independence. Until recently, they only entered into the affairs of Estrea when nonhuman survival was at stake, and only then if the cause was magical."

"Why then?" asked Bertram.

"Good question," said Sage. "You know that dragons evolved from the Ribendi, an earlier species closely related to them. The Ribendi had no magic. It wasn't necessary since the Ribendi were non-corporeal. I guess you could say they had their own powers, and without bodies, they wouldn't need the magic that humans might. Their powers had allowed them to travel to lots of different worlds, I guess. I wish we knew more about them and their travels. But there aren't any records from them. We can only guess at why they stayed here, what attracted them to Estrea. All we can say is that something here, maybe the land itself, attracted them. Or maybe it was that the society at the time was more caring and kind.

"We also don't know much about the appearance of the dragons. We can only guess that as the evolution occurred and as dragons became part of this world, magic began appearing. In this room alone, we have a number of different species who are telepathic, for instance. Not all squirrels or foxes, dogs or cats, are telepathic, but more and more seem to be developing the skill as the need arises. I've been following this, and Althea and I think that need is the primary cause for new talents arising."

Ty said, "I agree. We have telepathic cats in Dragonwind, where I'm from, and just recently we had a situation where a young girl was injured by bullies, and as a result, she lost her sight. But then a kitten came to the house where she was staying, and, well, for lack of a better word, she literally became Stella's eyes. Thanks to Mittens, Stella can see whatever Mittens sees. I've never heard of anything like that before."

"Exactly," said Sage. "So back to the dragons and isolation. The dragons did not help or interfere, depending on your perspective, unless magic was involved, and that magic was being used to harm others. Dragons feel responsible for the magic on this planet. Rightly or wrongly, they believe that it wouldn't have developed without dragon influence."

"So when we had to deal with The Wraith," said Esme, who had been very involved with that disaster, "the dragons helped us to save the planet."

"Precisely," said Sage.

The room was quiet as everyone thought back to that time when The Wraith was actively inhabiting bodies and wreaking havoc on their community. They would never have been able to defeat that creature and ultimately destroy it without the dragons' assistance.

After a few moments, Jasper said excitedly, "But the dragons are living in our world now because of Bergamen's mother, Windsong, who helped me save her son, when he was still in the egg. She knew what was going to happen in the future, and she knew that dragons and humans needed to bond again to save this world."

Sage laughed and said, "Yes, Jasper, and I'm glad now to have the chance to get to know both you and Bergamen since you two, as well as Bergamen's grandmother, Sapphire, are really making a difference."

Criseda spoke then. "Unfortunately, not everyone sees it that way."

"Very true," said Sage, "and that's why my husband was so excited when one of the other barons, a man named Zythrym, gave him a copy of the original treaty. He'd been fuming about not having an actual copy, as he knew his family's stories about it wouldn't be enough, but now he has a copy. Once he had that, he was overjoyed. He's going to enforce it to the letter."

"Well, I'll just cancel that provision of the treaty," said Bertram.

But then Bertram immediately shook his head, no doubt remembering all the changes to the monarchy that he'd made years ago, changes that would make that impossible. He now had a council that could overrule him because he never wanted absolute power. When he'd first become king at the age of eighteen, he'd realized that he had no experience, and he was also very tired of greedy, power-hungry monarchs such as what his uncle tried to be after Bertram's father had been killed. So he'd changed how this land was governed. He set up a council of advisors, but his very inexperience had led to the council being composed of barons, including very rich landowners and businessmen. Over the years, he'd done his best to diversify and expand that council, but it still had rich barons for over half of its members.

"I'll add more to the council then," said Bertram as he tried to come up with a quick solution to the problem.

Ty said, "That will defeat your purpose in making a more responsible government. You have redefined the council's powers in an effort to accomplish that, making for a more equal balance in power. You have allowed the council to override your decisions if most of them agree. Only if they don't do you still have the final say. And while it would take all of the barons being in total agreement now that you've added some of us to your advisory council, the barons still have a slim majority. You don't have absolute power, but you have considerably more than they do. We'd need to convince at least two barons to our side of the argument, which will take time."

"And don't forget, the majority of our population is very happy with the new changes," said Raymond. "I think that a number of years ago, the general population was leery of both magic and dragons. But things have gotten a lot better, and once the slum area was cleared, well, it seems to me that most of the population realizes how much they have benefited from both the dragons and those with magic. So I don't think you should change things just to accommodate greedy, power-hungry men."

Lance looked at his mother and said, "Isn't what we're doing—helping people get jobs and housing, learning to read and write—isn't that all good?"

Elicia, who headed the task force to do all that, put a hand on Lance's shoulder and said, "Yes, dear, it is. And I'm really glad you and Raymond are a part of this. You are both kind and using power wisely. Unfortunately, not everyone thinks the way we do."

"My father certainly doesn't. He continues to enslave his workers, and he won't be told that he can't do it," said Illyra.

"We'll just have to make him," said Lance.

Bertram looked at his son and said, "Your heart is in the right place, Lance, and I'm very proud of both you and Raymond. But this isn't going to be a quick fix. Our first plan has to be to keep the dragons safe from hunters."

"We can defend ourselves," said Oscar.

Foster said, "We certainly can. However, that could end up with the complete annihilation of the hunters, and that wouldn't go down well. Dragons killing is never a good plan."

Everyone was quiet for a time. Finally, Bertram said, "We have until Saturday morning to come up with a plan. That gives us two full days."

Ty said, "I think the dragons should at least get out of the capital. We can go to Dragonwind, which is almost part of the Aerie. If we're out of sight, that may help cooler heads to prevail."

Oscar said, "I agree. Fen, Edward, Foster, and I will leave today, and Jasper, you and Bergamen should do the same."

"Thank you all," said Bertram. "I should have realized that bringing the dragons into a more prominent role—especially when they were so willing to break up the slums, something I'd been trying to figure out how to do for years without success—was going to make those who profit from the misery of others very angry."

"True," said Ty. "In the past we've punished some of the wealthy, but overall, the structure of our society as well as the buildings and so forth have remained unchanged. The remaking of the slum area as well as Elicia's new committee have brought about very real, positive changes. Those who were happy with the old system are now going to fight back."

Fen said, "Well, we will stop them!"

With that decision reached, the meeting broke up.

CHAPTER 4

New Beginnings

Illyra stayed in her chair, glad that it was off to the side of the room, nearly in a corner, and watched as everyone stood and tried to decide what to do for the afternoon. Illyra felt uncertain, not really knowing most of these individuals, and not knowing what to do now. She'd been so focused on getting to the palace, giving the documents to the king, and then making sure her mother was rescued that she'd not thought beyond all that.

Now, as she watched the group moving forward, she felt alone and lost. The queen was talking to her mother, explaining what quarters she'd set aside for Sage and asking what they could do to help her settle in. Illyra was really happy that Sage finally had a friend and the support she needed. Sage would no longer be so isolated.

Illyra watched those who were her age. She saw Fen move to chat with Esme and Jasper. She realized that they were close friends, and she suspected they had already been through a lot together. Then she saw Raymond and Lance move to talk with the three of them, and she heard Raymond say, "It sounds as if you're all in a lot of danger. I guess I don't understand people like these barons."

Esme then chuckled and said with heavy sarcasm, "Danger? Really?" Then she looked at Raymond before saying more seriously, "Yes, once more we are being attacked. And like you, I don't really understand why people have to be like this."

Jasper added, "But we will fix this. I, for one, won't let anything happen to Bergamen."

Bergamen said, "And I'll protect you as well. It's important to remember that we're in this together."

At that moment, Illyra noticed that Ty and the king were coming over to her. She looked up at them as Ty said, "Illyra, would you and Chauncey like to come with us to consult with Aloysius? I would ask your mother, but she wouldn't be able to get up the long, winding stairs to Aloysius's library."

"Certainly," said Illyra as she stood, her hand on Chauncey's back.

As she did so, she saw Oscar looking her way. He nodded to her when he saw she was with the king and Ty, then he said, "You know that your room is waiting for you at our place. We'll check in with you this afternoon."

Suddenly, Illyra didn't feel so alone and lost. She smiled at Oscar and said, "Sounds great." Then she followed the king and Ty out of the room.

They walked down a long hallway until they came to a door, which Ty opened. She saw that it led to a narrow, winding staircase. As they climbed, Ty said, "Aloysius really doesn't want to be disturbed, and he wants his records just where he knows where they all are, so he's happy in his turret at the top of this staircase. But if we find things that others need to see, he can bring what's needed downstairs."

Bertram chuckled. "That will happen, once we give him the basic information, because not only will we want your mother's help but also Driselda's, and no way could a dragon of any size get up this staircase, much less a dragon as big as Driselda."

"And Aloysius is very fond of discussing history with Driselda," added Ty. "But we won't need all of Aloysius's records, so this is just an initial foray to alert him to the situation."

After climbing up four flights of stairs, they finally arrived at the top. King Bertram knocked on the door and then opened it, saying, "Aloysius, we need to let you know what's happened and find out what you know about ancient history."

An elderly man with white hair was bent over a manuscript. At their entrance he looked up, surprised to see people. "What did you say? Ancient history? Come in, come in."

Illyra looked around the very cluttered room and wondered where they could safely stand, but neither Ty nor Bertram seemed at all surprised by the clutter. They found their way carefully to the side of Aloysius's desk, and Bertram placed a copy of the treaty that Illyra had brought to him in front of Aloysius. As he did so, he said, "What can you tell us about this?"

Aloysius pushed his wire-frame glasses firmly up on his nose and looked at the document. After a few minutes, he said, "I thought I had the only copy of this. Where did you get it?"

Bertram introduced Illyra and then told Aloysius how they came to possess another copy of the treaty. Then he said, "We need to find a way to modify or change this treaty. As we understand it, this gives humans the right to hunt dragons if they leave the Aerie."

"Very true, unfortunately," said Aloysius. "And it also gives them the right to hunt any humans who moved to the Aerie in the beginning, as well as all their descendants in perpetuity."

"What!" exclaimed Ty.

"You heard me, young man," said Aloysius with impatience as he ran his hand through his hair. "This is a very badly drawn up treaty. I could read you a passage from the ancient historian, Tobias, to explain what happened, but I'll summarize, as I suspect time is of the essence.

"This treaty should never have been executed, but at the time, the dragons were so crushed by the way a small group of humans turned on them that they didn't care what happened to them. It's amazing what a small group of disgruntled, greedy, power-hungry people can do to ruin things for everyone else.

"Tobias said that after all the dragons had done to help humans over several centuries, they just lost all hope at this betrayal, not caring about anything, and retreated to the Aerie. At that time, it was the worst parcel of land on the entire planet, and no one wanted it. So the land was granted to the dragons, but the humans doing this wanted to be sure that the dragons could never leave that spot. That's why the hunting clauses were put in.

"And all the dragons signed it because at that time they were certain that they would never want to leave, and equally certain that they'd have nothing to do with most humans. And they kept to that plan for generations. They worked their rocky ground into a place that suited their needs, helped by a handful of humans who became bonded dragon riders."

"But now things have changed," said Bertram.

Aloysius nodded and said, "Lots of things have changed. But unfortunately, human greed and desire for power hasn't. You've made many changes during your reign to make our society more equitable, and I suspect that has angered those who were profiting from the old system. The biggest changes have been very recent, within the last year or so. Most of your subjects are thrilled with what you have accomplished. But the very wealthy, namely the barons, are used to wielding all the power, advising you, and getting their own way. They were fine with your earlier attempts to get rid of the slums, since all that really happened was a shift in who profited from them."

"But when the dragons helped destroy the slums and tunnels," began Bertram in a thoughtful voice, "they were enraged. The changes we made last year and the community help that Elicia and her committee continue to offer have really transformed our country, but I guess it was bound to upset the richest and most powerful."

"Yes," said Aloysius. "Change is always a bit problematic, but this change more so than most because it involved not only you and your wife, but also those who wield magical abilities and, even more so, the dragons—another species, and one that centuries ago was shoved aside as being nothing more than animals. The fact that they were instrumental in the solution to a problem the wealthy barons never saw as a problem, and which they see as a direct attack on them personally, has just inflamed the issue beyond all belief."

"But can't we stop this?" asked Ty.

"Unfortunately," said Aloysius, "this treaty was never revoked or amended. It is just as legal now as it was the day it was written."

"We have to be able to do something," said King Bertram with obvious desperation in his voice.

Aloysius studied the treaty carefully while Illyra, Ty, and Bertram watched. Finally, Aloysius looked up, and there was the hint of a smile on his face. He said, "They were very specific about whom they could kill," he began. "For instance, all three of you could be killed, as you all are descendants of the original dragon riders. In addition, it is now relatively easy to tell if someone is a descendant by whether or not they have magic."

"But my children don't have any magic," said the king.

"No, and you only have a weak telepathy," agreed Aloysius. "However, they are your children. You could try to deny that, but one look at them would prove their ancestry even if you were so inclined. And Driselda says that while magic can skip several generations, it does have a way of reappearing in times of need. You only need to look at Esme and yourself, Ty, to see that."

"OK," said Ty. "So, what can we do to prevent a blood bath?"

Aloysius let out a chuckle and said, "Well, while they were extremely precise in listing who could be killed for leaving the Aerie, they were very lax in defining the Aerie itself. I suspect this is because they wanted to be able to define that land in ways that would allow them the greatest latitude in killing residents. So they just said, 'the top of the mountain.'"

The group thought of the topography of the Aerie, with its craggy out-croppings indistinguishable from the rest of the mountain. They realized that this made the dragons especially vulnerable.

"How does that help us?" asked Illyra.

"It means," said Ty, figuring out what Aloysius meant, "that a case could be made for Dragonwind being a part of the Aerie, doesn't it? After all, Dragonwind is at the top of the mountain, just about a mile below the Aerie, but still up in the mountain, a good four hours up from the capital."

Aloysius smiled and said, "Yes, the dragons could annex the village of Dragonwind, if the residents of Dragonwind agreed."

"What would that take, to make it legal?" asked Bertram.

"I would suggest that if the residents of Dragonwind voted to secede from Estrea and ask to be admitted to the Aerie, that you, sire, could agree."

"It isn't necessarily the total solution to the problem," said Bertram. "But it would protect a lot of magical beings since Dragonwind has the largest population of those with magic, and Blossom, Criseda, and Bergamen already live there. Oscar and Foster have a second cave in Dragonwind and could move back with Fen and Edward. It would stop the immediate carnage."

"Criseda and I will leave immediately for Dragonwind," said Ty. "I'm pretty sure the residents will support this. We'll also talk with Sapphire, since she, as leader of the dragons, will have to agree to the annexation."

"And see if Driselda has any other documents or ideas," said Aloysius.

"Meanwhile," said Bertram, "I'll plan for the evacuation of any in the capital who are in danger, including my family."

"And you, sire," said Ty. "You're their number-one target."

"Yes, I suppose," said Bertram reluctantly.

Aloysius said, "If I may be so bold as to suggest it, even with all the changes you have made, you still have the right to decide where the seat of government will be. You could make Dragonwind the capital of Estrea, at least for now. Then if the barons want to conduct any business, they will have to travel to Dragonwind."

King Bertram chuckled before saying, "And they will be searched for any weapons before being allowed to enter. That's a great idea, Aloysius. You are quite crafty and devious!"

"I'm here to serve, sire," said Aloysius with a smile. "I would also like to be taken to Dragonwind so I can oversee the documents necessary to make all this legal. We can't afford to miss any of the finer points."

King Bertram smiled and said, "You and Driselda will make sure we have a strong legal fortress."

"Criseda and I will let you know when we have both the villagers' and the dragons' permission for the annexation, sire," Ty said. "And may I suggest that you begin the evacuation first thing in the morning? It might only take four hours on horseback, but loaded wagons filled with supplies and evacuees will take longer to arrive in Dragonwind. Even if the paperwork isn't entirely complete by the time the wagons arrive, it will make you all easier to protect. The dragons aren't going to roll over this time."

"I agree, Ty," said Bertram.

With that, Ty bolted down the stairs and took off on Criseda.

▲

Once Illyra, Chauncey, and Bertram left the tower, Bertram went to find his wife and family. Illyra wasn't sure where to go now. She looked around the hallway but didn't see anyone. She was trying to remember just how she had entered the palace, thinking that she could go back to Oscar and Foster's cave. After all, they had invited her to continue staying with them. But that would require her to pass through the family room where Bertram had just gone to be with his family.

Just then the family room door opened, and Oscar, Foster, and Fen, with Edward, came out, followed by Esme and her bonded creatures, followed by Jasper and Bergamen. Oscar said, "Ah, good, there you are, Illyra. We plan to go back to our cave and get something to eat and plan for our departure from the capital. Please come with us."

Illyra smiled and said, "Thank you. I would like that."

Oscar walked over to a small doorway, which Illyra discovered led right out into the backyard. The group headed to the back gate and the path through the forest to the dragons' cave. Once there, everyone settled in the great room. Fen and Jasper offered to make lunch, and while they were do-ing that, Oscar said, "So we're all heading back to Dragonwind no later than tomorrow morning."

Fen, still working in the kitchen, said, "There are so many magical beings now, and most of them are in Dragonwind, so it does make sense to keep us all together. And it will be easier for everyone to be protected."

"I guess," said Oscar, "but it does feel as if we are running away."

"Nonsense," said Foster. "We could certainly take on those barons. They have no idea what dragons can do. But a lot of humans would get killed, and I don't think that's at all what Bertram, or indeed any of us, wants."

"And there are weaker, smaller beings who need our protection," said Bergamen.

Samantha the squirrel said, *I hope you aren't talking about us.*

Edward the fox added, *Because that would be really insulting. Bring these jerks on. We can handle them.*

Rupert the fox said, *Hear, hear. That's right.*

Bergamen held up a claw and said, "Hang on. I wasn't meaning to insult anyone. But what about, for instance, Stella? She's only seven and blind, and yes, she has her cat, Mittens, but she's still a kitten. And there are others. I suspect from what Bertram was saying as we left the family room that he will have his whole family come, and that will include Ernest and the twins, who don't have magic of their own and who also don't have bonded creatures."

Bergamen is correct. We all need to go to a place where we can help defend everyone, said Chauncey, *and from what I understand about Aloysius's plan, the goal is to make Dragonwind part of the Aerie and therefore safe for us all.*

"Really?" said Oscar. "I hadn't heard that yet, but it makes sense."

"Ty and Criseda hope to convince the villagers to agree to leave Estrea and become part of the Aerie," said Illyra. "I've never been to Dragonwind, but the plan makes sense."

Esme said, "Oh, Dragonwind is a wonderful place! You'll love it."

Fen came over with a tray loaded with sandwiches, which he placed on the coffee table. Jasper had another tray with tea for everyone. Everyone settled into lunch, and Jasper, Fen, and Esme told Illyra all about Dragonwind.

Illyra ate her sandwich and watched the others. She'd never experienced anything like the friendships she saw here. It had always been just her and her mother. This new environment was confusing and yet comforting. It would take some getting used to, but she was beginning to think that it would be a good situation.

CHAPTER 5

DRAGONWIND

Ty and Criseda landed on the village green in Dragonwind. All around them they saw quaint, wood-framed buildings in shades of blue and yellow; the streets were paved with cobblestones. The village itself was nestled in the mountains and surrounded by forests. Martha, a short, heavyset woman in her late fifties with gray hair and eyes and a kind, plump face, and her partner, Kyle, a tall, solidly built man with hazel eyes, nearly white hair, and a gray beard, came out of Martha's bakery, located on the north side of the village green, and walked over to Ty and Criseda.

"Hi, Ty," said Martha. "We weren't expecting you. Are you OK?"

"Actually, no," said Ty. "Something has happened, and I need to call a town meeting right away."

Ty was not only a roving ambassador for King Bertram, but also the leader of Dragonwind.

"Oh, of course," said Martha.

"Why don't you and Criseda fly over the village and call for everyone to come to the town center," suggested Kyle. "I think that would be the fastest way to alert everyone."

"Good idea," said Ty as he vaulted back onto Criseda.

Martha said, "Come back here after you've done that, and I'll fix you lunch while people gather."

"Will do, and thanks," said Ty as Criseda took off.

Dragonwind in fact was a small mountain village located just southeast of and below the dragons' Aerie. As Ty and Criseda flew over it, Criseda, with the louder voice, called out, "Village meeting in the town hall now. Come, everyone; come now to the town hall."

The two of them circled the village three times with this message before they again landed on the village green. Ty walked into Martha's cottage, which was next to the bakery, sat at her kitchen table, and ate a bowl of stew as well as some freshly baked bread that Martha placed in front of him. As he ate, he told Martha and Kyle about the ancient treaty. They were horrified. While neither of them had any magical gifts, Martha was the legal guardian for Esme, Jasper, and Lyra, as well as being Ty's former guardian, and she and Kyle cared greatly for their foster kids.

"What can be done?" Martha asked as Ty finished his lunch.

Ty stood up and took his dishes over to the sink. He said, "The king is trying to find a legal solution that won't result in a massacre. That's why Criseda and I are here. And Criseda has asked Sapphire, as the leader of the dragons, and Driselda, as the dragon historian, to come to our meeting."

Kyle and Martha also stood as Martha said, "We'd better get over to the town hall, then."

The three of them walked out of Martha's cottage, which was on the northwest corner of a row of buildings, and headed past the bakery and on to the large building next door to the bakery and also on the north side of the green. As they did so, a gorgeous bluish-purple dragon landed on the village green, followed by a large emerald-green dragon. They joined Criseda and headed for the village hall as well.

"Thanks for coming," said Ty when he caught up to the dragons.

"Criseda has briefed us, and this is a major crisis," said Sapphire.

"Never in all my years as a historian," said Driselda, "did I ever think this ancient treaty would be resurrected. We are going to rue the day we just folded under the hatred of a few humans."

Sapphire said, "Honestly, I never thought we'd have any meaningful relationships with humans ever again after our banishment, but now that things have changed, I certainly wouldn't want them to go back to the way they were."

"Hopefully they won't," said Ty.

They entered the village hall, and Ty was pleased to see that lots of the villagers were already here. He even saw that Tyler, the pharmacist who lived in the neighboring village of Rocking Rocks, was here.

"Hi, Tyler," Ty said. "What brings you here?"

"I was bringing some medicines here for some of my patients and decided I'd better find out what's going on."

"Excellent," said Ty. "This could affect Rocking Rocks as well."

Rocking Rocks was a village a bit smaller than Dragonwind, also located up in the mountains, about ten miles northeast of Dragonwind.

Ty walked to the podium at the front of the hall and called out to everyone. "I'm glad you all could come at such short notice," he said, and the room immediately went quiet. Ty began. "You all know about the changes that the king and queen have brought to the capital: clearing the slum area, setting up schools not only for children and young adults, but also for any who can't read, helping with job placement, and so on."

People nodded, and someone said, "They've done a wonderful job."

"However, it turns out that a group of wealthy barons are enraged by all the changes since the renovation of the slums. They feel as if it has cut into their profits and limited their power, something they will not tolerate."

There was general laughter at this, and Ty went on. "Unfortunately, they have unearthed an ancient treaty, from the time when humans turned on the dragons and banished them to the Aerie."

Ty went on to explain about the terms, including the hunting provisions. He was glad to see that the villagers were properly horrified by this news.

"That can't be allowed," said Jeb, Ty's best friend and the gamekeeper and warden for the forests around Dragonwind.

"King Bertram and Aloysius think they've found a loophole, if you all agree," said Ty. "The treaty is very specific about the right to kill dragons, as well as any humans who have bonded or sided with dragons, if they leave the Aerie. But what they weren't very specific about was the exact boundaries of the Aerie. So what we're proposing, if you're in favor, is that Dragonwind secedes from Estrea and instead becomes a part of the Aerie," concluded Ty.

Jeb said, "So in effect, we make the Aerie's land larger."

"Yes," said Ty. "There are a lot of bonded pairs right here in Dragonwind who would be in danger if we don't."

"Do the dragons want us?" someone in the back of the room asked.

Ty nodded to Sapphire, who spoke. "Many of you may remember that I was reluctant to have the dragons involved in human affairs unless other species were being harmed by human actions.

"But since the birth of my grandson, Bergamen, and our closer alliance, all of the dragons have truly been touched by our friendship with all of you. I think our world is a better place when we work together to provide for all. So yes, we would be honored if you wanted to be included in our borders."

Cheers rose from the group, and finally Kyle said, "So, what do we have to do to make this official?"

"King Bertram, Alloysius, and others from the capital will be here by tomorrow afternoon, and we'll draw up the actual documents. Driselda, we'd like you to help with any knowledge you have of the original treaty," said Ty.

"After Criseda contacted me about this, I immediately searched out our copy of the treaty, and unfortunately those rich barons are correct. I will, of course, go through all our records," said Driselda.

"Thanks," said Ty.

"So, what do we have to do to make this legal?" asked Jeb.

"That's why I've called the meeting," said Ty. "We need to vote as a village to join the Aerie, and then the dragons need to vote to annex us."

"And if that happens, then Paul and Wilhelmina will be safe?" asked Paul's mother, Naomi.

Sapphire smiled and said, "Yes, and so would all the other bonded pairs and dragons living in Dragonwind."

Martha said, "That's great."

Blossom, a pink female dragon who was the best healer among the dragons, said, "Excellent! I love my cave on the edge of Dragonwind, and Martha and I work well together."

Ty said, "All we need to do now is to put this to the vote. All those in favor of joining with the Aerie, raise your hands."

Ty looked around the room as every single hand went up. He'd never been prouder of his village than he was at this moment.

Everyone cheered the results, and Sapphire then said, "I'm sure the dragons will vote to expand their boundaries as well."

Ty said, "And we'll draw up the formal document tomorrow. Driselda, maybe you could draw up a temporary document today after the dragons vote, and Sapphire and I can sign it, just so we're sure we're legal from today forward."

Tyler then raised his hand, and Ty said, "Yes, Tyler."

"Thanks, Ty," Tyler said. "I want to know if Rocking Rocks can do the same thing. I know we don't have nearly as many bonded pairs, but we are very close to Dragonwind, geographically, socially, and economically."

Ty looked over at Sapphire, who nodded and said, "I see no objections to that. We'd be happy to have you."

"You just need to get your villagers to vote, and if they do, then we'll be sure you're on the document tomorrow," said Ty.

"If they do vote to join, I'll write something up today as well," said Tyler.

With that, the meeting broke up. As the villagers left the town hall, there was lots of excited chatter, with comments like, "So we'll be living in the Aerie, and we didn't even have to move. That's pretty cool."

Once the villagers had left the meeting, Sapphire suggested that Ty and Criseda come up to the Aerie and meet with the dragons. Ty agreed, and so Sapphire, Driselda, Blossom, and Criseda with Ty flew the mile northwest to the Aerie. The Aerie was located at the top of the mountain and contained a ring of caves, along with several flat areas where livestock grazed. It wasn't a large area, but it was enough to sustain the dragons independently, so they didn't have to rely on humans.

Sapphire called a meeting of those living in the Aerie. Then Driselda presented the situation, saying, "In a way, this is our doing, since we didn't fight the humans who exiled us. We never should have agreed to the hunting, and now not only are we in danger, but so are all our human friends who have been gifted with magic."

Driselda continued to explain, and once the dragons understood not only what had happened but also that dragons were actually responsible for the current situation because they had just given up to a handful of humans, they immediately voted to accept both Dragonwind and Rocking Rocks into their boundaries. It all made sense because the two communities were closely allied, Dragonwind having helped Rocking Rocks rebuild and resettle an area that had once been simply abandoned mines. And the two were also geographically relatively close, just ten miles apart.

"Thank you all," said Ty. "We will get this sorted. Ultimately we can't allow a small group of greedy, power-hungry men to dominate Estrea, but at least for now, we should be able to avoid a bloodbath of innocent creatures."

Sapphire nodded and said, "We never should have allowed that hunting clause into the treaty. And my daughter, Windsong, was very clear that she saw the need for dragons to work with other species, including humans. I suspect that she saw more dangers than those we've already overcome, so we need to become a society that pulls together."

"I agree," said Ty. "I also know that is not what these barons want, so first we have to deal with them!"

"I don't envy you," said Sapphire, "but rest assured, the dragons will protect our newly enlarged Aerie and all those within our borders, no matter what the species."

"Thanks, Sapphire," said Ty. "Criseda and I will go back to the capital to help with the evacuations. Refugees from the capital, including the royal family as well as Illyra and Sage, will arrive tomorrow. See you then."

CHAPTER 6

EVACUATION

Ty and Criseda arrived back at the palace late that evening. They went to King Bertram's office to report.

After greeting the king, Ty sat in one of the chairs as Criseda sat on the floor next to him. Ty then said, "We were successful, and in fact, Tyler, the pharmacist from Rocking Rocks, asked if his village could also be included, and Sapphire agreed."

"That's wonderful," said Bertram. "They aren't in as much danger because there are fewer residents there who have magic, but it will be two villages seceding from Estrea, which might put more pressure on the barons."

"Also, Driselda and Sapphire are determined to fix what they see as the dragons' mistake when they agreed to the treaty all those years ago," said Ty.

"We do want this fixed," said Bertram, "but I don't think the dragons are responsible. I'd say the way humans turned on the dragons, who had been nothing but kind to them, is the greatest crime, as it is a complete betrayal on so many levels."

"How are the plans for the move to Dragonwind going?" Ty asked.

"We will have the wagons heading to Dragonwind before dawn tomorrow. That should get everyone to Dragonwind by early afternoon, even with the steep climb into the mountains. I know the trails are narrow and winding in a number of locations, which will make it harder on the horses and wagons.

Still, we should all have plenty of time to settle into whatever accommodations the villagers can provide for us," said Bertram.

"I've talked to Martha and Kyle and some of the other villagers, and they are going to fix up the town hall for the new arrivals. Kyle and Wilson, our lead carpenter, are busy even now putting together portable walls so the large room can be divided up."

"Great," said Bertram. "And I'm having portable camp beds and bedding brought in the wagons, along with a plentiful supply of food and other necessities. I don't want the villagers to have to give from their own supplies."

"It is going to be hardest on those from the capital, especially since we have no idea just how long this exile is going to have to last," said Ty.

"I plan to let my council know that I'm calling an emergency meeting for Monday in Dragonwind," said Bertram. "That will give them the weekend to figure out their own transportation."

"And I assume you are also going to mention that there won't be any hunting allowed in the Aerie and give them the new boundaries for the dragons' land," said Ty with a chuckle.

King Bertram smiled and said, "Definitely. I am prepared to move the seat of government to Dragonwind, even if it will be technically outside Estrea's boundaries until this can be resolved. Maybe Sapphire and I can declare that Dragonwind is neutral, belonging to both of us. The barons won't like that, but they will have the choice either to quit the council or act reasonably. It will be their choice. My family and I are very fond of Dragonwind and its inhabitants."

"What about the palace?" asked Ty. "Are you worried about leaving it empty?"

"I've already talked with the palace guard, and Simion is quite sure that his company will be able to keep any intruders out of the palace. I don't think there is any danger there, and I think that we will find the shifting of the government to be much less disrupting than the barons will. After all, they have businesses to run and employees to keep enslaved."

"Very true," said Ty. "What is the makeup of your council? I don't remember the exact numbers."

"Well, I did put you and Criseda, Esme, and Jasper and Bergamen on the council. I was going to add more individuals from the renovated area along with some more shop owners, but I haven't managed that yet. And of course there is the group of barons, Fergus and his cronies. There are nine of them in the council of fourteen, so they can vote anything down or change things as they wish. I do have the power of the veto, but unfortunately, any changes to the treaty would have to be ratified by a majority of the council."

Ty thought of Fergus's past actions and cringed at what he was capable of. He had been one of the worst landlords, but just never managed to get caught as some of the others had. In fact, he wasn't one of the richest when the first attempts at cleaning up the slums was attempted. But he took over properties as fast as the king had removed corrupt money lenders, so that now he was one of the richest and most powerful of the group. Certainly, he and his cronies would never ratify any changes.

"Hmm," said Ty. "That is a problem then."

"We'll figure it out. Remember, Bergamen's mother said that Estrea was going to need dragons and humans working together to stop some calamity. It's not clear what that emergency will be, but I trust her foretelling. We need to get this old treaty nullified before that happens."

"I agree," said Ty. "The only thing that's going to stop the barons is something that costs them money or power."

Early the next morning, they reconvened to see to the final details for the evacuation. As they were planning, Henry entered the office and said, "A very irate Fergus is demanding to see you."

Fergus pushed the steward aside and yelled, "Where is my family?"

King Bertram said very calmly, "Would you care to have a seat?"

"No, I wouldn't," said Fergus. "I want my wife and my daughter, now."

"That's not possible," said King Bertram, still using a very calm voice.

"Why not?" yelled Fergus. "They're under my control. Bring them here right now."

"Illyra is of age now, so she is her own person and can go where she wants," began Bertram.

"No, she can't," said Fergus. "I've promised her in marriage to Lord Carl Humphrey."

"Did Illyra agree to this?" asked Bertram.

"I haven't told her yet," said Fergus, "but she will do as she is told."

"No, she won't," said Bertram. "The choice is hers, and given that Lord Carl is old enough to be her grandfather, or even great-grandfather, I can't imagine she'd agree."

"She'll agree," said Fergus. "She has no say in the matter. I arrange my affairs as I see fit, and she will obey me. And my wife will do the same. She's a cripple and unable to care for herself."

During this heated exchange, Ty and Criseda just watched in amazement. Ty spoke to Criseda. *How does this jerk manage to deal with anyone? Why would anyone put up with him?*

Criseda said, *I have no idea. I wonder if he has some sort of hold over the other barons. I can't imagine anyone likes him.*

King Bertram held up a hand to stop Fergus's outburst and said, "Your wife has requested sanctuary, and it has been granted since there is compelling evidence that her so-called accident was actually attempted murder. She says she's only stayed with you for the past three years to protect Illyra until she came of age, which she has now done."

"You can't believe that stupid bird," said Fergus. "He's only a dumb animal."

"On the contrary," said Bertram, "I find Star's evidence of not only Sage's fall but also many of your other activities to be very compelling."

"B-b-b-ut," stuttered Fergus.

"Now I am glad you are here so I can let you know what's been happening after your threats to murder dragons and those with magic who leave the Aerie."

"It's all perfectly legal," snarled Fergus. "I ought to know, as the terms of that treaty have been known by my family for generations, ever since my great-great-great-grandfather helped write it and got it signed. And now I have an indisputable copy. I never needed to have it enforced until you started trying to integrate dragons into our country. You're directly responsible for bringing the enforcement of this treaty into the present moment."

"I know that your plans are within the terms of the treaty. Just be very sure that you do follow the law," said the king. "All dragons are now in the

Aerie, and by the end of tomorrow, all those descended from the original dragon riders will also be. The Aerie's boundaries have also been extended to protect the villages of Dragonwind and Rocking Rocks. And as you say that it's my fault that the treaty is now going to be enforced, I'd say that your distant ancestor is responsible for the very sloppy way the boundaries of the Aerie were defined. It is that sloppiness that is allowing the boundaries to be shifted."

"What!" said Fergus. "You can't do that."

"I think you'll find out that individual villages and towns are permitted to decide where they may have higher allegiance. Both villages have petitioned to leave Estrea and to join the Aerie. I have agreed to the secessions, as is my right as head of Estrea, and Sapphire has welcomed them, as is her right as the leader of the Aerie."

"Well, that means you have to go there," said Fergus, a smug look on his face.

"True," said Bertram. "So starting now, all council meetings will be held in Dragonwind. And I'm calling an emergency meeting for Monday afternoon, in Dragonwind, to discuss the changes in the ancient treaty."

"But how is that possible?" asked Fergus.

"You'll find it is all legal," said Bertram, "and obviously this situation has to be changed. You and the other barons can find your own way to Dragonwind, and you will arrive for the discussion and a binding vote, according to our laws and traditions."

As the king watched a sneaky look pass across Fergus's face, Bertram added, "And you all will arrive unarmed. No weapons will be permitted, and you will be searched before you are allowed to enter the village."

Fergus yelled, "You can't do this!"

Ty and Criseda stood then as Ty said, "You know, you brought this onto yourself. You're the one who has always bullied people, including your family. You're the one who threatened the dragons simply because you didn't want the slums cleared up. As I'm sure you will find out all too soon, you are on the losing side in all this. Your family has already found sanctuary, and most of the citizens of Estrea are really happy with the new order of things in the capital. Other areas will be hoping to follow suit, I'm sure."

Ty was quite confident that all the efforts of the past year to remake the society of Estrea, especially with all the help offered to most of the population, would result in people turning against the likes of Fergus.

"Well, my workers won't," said Fergus.

Ty just smiled, very confident that anyone who worked for a bully like Fergus would be among the first to switch sides.

King Bertram now stood and said, "This discussion is at an end. I'll leave it up to you to let the other eight council members know about the emergency meeting. I've already let Ty, Criseda, Esme, Jasper, and Bergamen know. See you at 1:00 p.m. on Monday."

Just then the office door opened, and Bertram said, "Henry, will you please show Fergus out?"

"Certainly, sire. This way, Baron," said Henry.

"You'll regret this," said Fergus as he stormed past Henry.

Henry gave a small bow to the king and followed Fergus out, closing the door as he went.

"Well, that was certainly unpleasant," said Ty.

"I agree," said Bertram, "but it had to be done. And notice of the emergency meeting has been given, so we are now free to leave."

There was a knock on the door, and Simion, the head of the palace guard, came in. "Sire, the wagons are loaded, and everyone is ready to depart. They are just waiting for you."

"We're coming now," said Bertram. "I hope you don't have any unpleasantness here at the palace during our exile."

"Please don't worry. My men and I will be able to handle the likes of Fergus and the other barons, should they decide to try anything. Everything will remain as it is, ready for your return."

"Thanks, Simion," said Bertram as he, Ty, and Criseda left.

▲

Once they were out in the courtyard, they discovered a convoy of six wagons, most of which were loaded with provisions as well as people. They could see Illyra and Chauncey sitting with the twins and Eugene being held by the queen as she sat next to Sage, who had Star on her left shoulder. Raymond was driving the second wagon and had Lance and Aloysius sitting on the bench with him. Oscar and Foster were there with Fen, who, with Edward, would ride on Oscar, and Esme, along with Samantha and Rupert, who would ride on Foster. Jasper was on Bergamen, of course.

King Bertram got up on the front wagon, next to his wife, and took the reins that one of the palace guards handed him. "Is everyone ready?"

"Yes," yelled his excited children.

"Then, tallyho!" said Bertram as the wagons moved out through the palace gates and turned north onto the road to Dragonwind. Once they'd cleared the gates, the dragons took flight. The wagons would take about four hours to get to Dragonwind, and during the trip, the dragons would act as patrols.

Ty had set things up so that the four dragons would fly to Dragonwind, where their passengers would be off-loaded so they could help the villagers prepare for the new arrivals. Jasper and Bergamen, as well as Ty and Fen, would stay in the village while Criseda, Oscar, and Foster flew back to the convoy to guard it all the way to the village.

Along the way, they passed rocky outcroppings and dense forests. The crisp, cool air delighted humans and dragons alike.

The wagons arrived soon after noon, and they were welcomed by the entire village on the village green. Everyone except Illyra and Sage had been here before, even Bertram and Elicia's youngest three, and it didn't take long before old friendships were renewed. Fen caught up with the five orphans ze'd rescued from the slums of the capital before it was rebuilt. The three boys—six-year-old Felix, nine-year-old Matthew, and six-year-old Robert—swarmed Fen. They were all being fostered by Naomi; her nearly nine-year-old son, Paul; and Paul's bonded moose, Wilhelmina.

Quickly demanding their chance to greet Fen were seven-year-olds Priscilla and Stella, along with their cats, Prince and Mittens, the latter of which was bonded to Stella and served as eyes for the blind girl. They were being fostered by Elfrida, a retired schoolteacher, and her partner, Agatha, an elderly blind lady who'd moved to Dragonwind from the capital to help Stella. Wilhelmina stood protectively over the group, with Paul at her side.

Meanwhile, Esme and Jasper gave Martha big hugs and said how glad they were to be home at least for a while. Martha fostered both of them—although at the moment they were spending more time helping at the palace—as she had done with Ty before he became an adult. Her other current foster, sixteen-year-old Lyra, gave Esme and Jasper each a hug and said how glad she was to see them.

Illyra seemed a bit lost, so Esme immediately brought her over to meet Lyra and Martha and then included her in the group clamoring for updates. Once the flurry of greetings started to subside, Martha called for order.

"Welcome, everyone!" she said. "We are so happy to have you all here. We've done the best that we can with accommodations. Many of you have spots here already. Kyle's and my home will once again be filled with teens, which suits us just fine. Esme with Rupert and Samantha, Lyra with Matilda, Jasper, and Bergamen will be with us. Aloysius, if you wish, Driselda would love to have you stay at the Aerie with her."

Aloysius saw the large dragon on the edge of the village green and waved happily to her as he walked over to stand with her.

Martha continued, "King Bertram, Queen Elicia, we've set up space at one end of the village hall for you and your family, and Blossom would like to offer space for Sage and Illyra in her cave, which is in the forest just past Elfrida and Agatha's home, which you can see there just behind the northwest corner of Martha's home. There will also be a large dining area at the other end of the hall where we can all gather for food and visiting. I hope that sounds good."

Queen Elicia took Martha by the hands and said, "Martha, whatever you provide will be wonderful."

Then she looked around at all the villagers as she said, "We are all so grateful to you all for welcoming us."

"Right then," said Kyle to a group of villagers. "Let's help these folks unload the wagons and get them all set up. Then I believe Martha and others have lunch for all of us."

It took the afternoon to get everyone settled. Blossom helped Illyra get Sage to the cave on the outskirts of the village. Chauncey went with them. Blossom told them, "This used to be Ty's cave, and then after he bonded with Criseda, the two of them and Ty's cat, Foxy, lived there. But then they found another cave directly north of the village, which is bigger and which they like better, so when I moved to the village from the Aerie, I asked if I could use it. It suits me well. And you'll appreciate the fact that it has running water. Ty fixed that up."

Blossom led them into the cave, helping Sage with her rolling chair. Then she said, "Sage, I hope you won't be offended, but I'd really like to see if I can help you. I'd also like Ty to look at you, as he has the gift of healing magic."

"I don't think there's anything anyone can do," said Sage.

"You won't know if we don't look," said a determined Blossom, "and I bet your husband never even tried to get you proper care."

Illyra spoke up and said, "You're right about that. Mom, let's get you examined."

Sage said, "OK, but don't get your hopes up."

Blossom sent a telepathic message to Ty. *Ty, can you come take a look at Sage when you have a moment?*

I can come now, he replied.

Blossom said, "Ty will be here shortly. Meanwhile, I'll examine you. Why don't you lie down on the bed in here," she added as she walked into a bedroom that was decorated in a pale shade of lavender, with a gorgeous lavender-and-pink quilt on a large bed. "I changed some of the decor after Ty moved out, but he's the one who actually shaped the cave. I think you'll find it very comfortable."

Illyra helped her mother to get onto the bed, and Blossom began her exam, testing Sage's mobility. After a few minutes, Ty arrived, and he continued with the exam. He put his hands on Sage's back and then asked her if she felt anything.

After a few minutes, Sage exclaimed, "You're sending heat into my body, aren't you?"

"Yes," said Ty, sounding pleased. He continued to work on Sage for nearly half an hour. Then he said, "Do you have any pain?"

Sage nodded and said, "Yes, quite a bit."

"Your vertebrae are out of alignment, and they are pinching nerves. That pressure on your nerves is causing both the paralysis and your pain. I'm going to try to adjust things. It may get worse before it gets better, but please bear with me."

"Do whatever you think is best," said Sage.

Illyra held one of her mother's hands, and Star watched from the edge of the bed. Illyra knew when it hurt her mother because her hand tightened, but Sage was quiet.

Patiently, Ty worked on Sage's spine, especially her lower spine. Finally, Ty straightened up and said, "How do you feel?"

"The pain is much, much better," said Sage. "Thank you!"

"Shall we see what's happening with the paralysis?" asked Ty. "Can you feel this?" he asked as he touched her toes on both feet.

"Yes," said Sage, almost shouting.

Ty looked at Illyra and smiled. Then he said, "Let's see what happens when we get her up."

Illyra and Ty helped her mother to sit up on the edge of the bed. Then Ty said, "Can you move your feet? Don't try to stand; just see if you can wiggle your feet."

Sage concentrated, and nothing happened for a few minutes. But then her feet began to wiggle.

"Mom, you did it," shouted Illyra joyfully.

Sage smiled at her and then looked at Ty. "I did it."

"Yes," said Ty. "You haven't walked since your accident, but I can now confirm that you didn't crack your spine. You bruised it badly, causing it to swell. There is still a fair amount of swelling, but I was able to reduce some of that, taking pressure off the nerves. It will take time, but I see no reason why you can't walk again."

Illyra threw her arms around her mother and then looked up at Ty and said, "How can we ever thank you?"

"I have sped the process of healing up. Healing magic is one of my gifts. But honestly, a competent doctor would have figured out the correct diagnosis. Your father should have gotten her proper medical treatment right after the accident."

Star then spoke. *Well, considering he was trying to kill her, I don't think that was ever going to happen.*

Ty looked at the raven and then back to Sage and Illyra. Finally, he said, "Is that true?"

Sage nodded and said, "Star saved my life by alerting the household to my fall, a fall caused when my husband pushed me down the stairs."

"Well, you're safe now. Bertram has granted both of you sanctuary, so Fergus won't be able to hurt you again," said Ty. "I'll let you rest now."

Blossom said, "I'll apply compresses to help with the swelling."

"Yes," said Ty, "and I'll work with her every day to help her get stronger."

Ty looked at Illyra and Chauncey and said, "Your mother should rest now. Would you like to come with me, and I'll show you around the village and introduce you both to Martha and the others?"

"That would be nice," said Illyra.

Can I meet the moose? asked Chauncey.

Ty laughed and said, "Definitely. Wilhelmina would love to meet you as well. Let's go."

They left the cave, and Ty led them down the path to the village green. He said, "That long building on the northeast side of the green contains both the village hall, where meals will be served and where the king's family will be housed, and next to that Martha's bakery, where you can always get great food. Then next to that is Martha's house, which at the moment is full to bursting as only Martha can want. Esme, Lyra, Jasper, and Bergamen are all staying there along with the two foxes and one squirrel. We have a lot of bonded pairs here, more than you'll find anywhere else. There are also more magical gifts, such as my healing, and we think that's because of our proximity to the Aerie."

They walked around the green, and Ty said, "That house just north of Martha's is Elfrida and Agatha's, and Priscilla and Stella are being fostered there, along with two cats."

They turned a corner and were face to face with the largest house in the village, located on the western side of the village green. Ty said, "That house is big because Wilhelmina lives there. Paul is bonded to Wilhelmina, and they live with Paul's mother, Naomi, who helps in the bakery. And Naomi is also fostering three boys that Fen rescued from the slum area before it was renovated. Chauncey, you'd be most welcome there, as would you, Illyra. It's a home that is filled with love and energy."

They kept going around the green, and just past Naomi's home there was a path that Ty said led to the Aerie about one mile to the northwest. They continued south, still on the east side of the green, and finally reached another path into the forest. Ty said, "My friend Jeb lives down this path in a small cottage. He is the game warden and forest steward. He and Kyle, along with Oscar, Foster, Criseda, and Bergamen, will be helping me to guard the village during this crisis, so please don't worry about your safety."

They continued along both the south and east ends of the green, where Ty pointed to the road leading south from the southeast corner, saying, "And of course that's the road to the capital," and they then turned north along the fourth side of the green, returning to the northeastern side of the village halls. They continued to the north, noticing first a new, well-traveled path as Ty said, "That path into the woods leads to Rocking Rocks, about ten miles to the northeast."

They continued north past the path, and Ty pointed to two caves, one west of them about five hundred feet behind the bakery and one about one hundred yards east of them as he said, pointing first to the left, "That one is the cave where I live with Criseda and my cat, Foxy." Then, pointing to the right, he said, "That one is the cave where Fen, Edward, Oscar, and Foster live when they are in Dragonwind. It's not quite as large or elaborate as their cave behind the palace, but it's a good spot."

"Dragonwind does seem to be a lovely place," said Illyra. She realized that there was a calm quiet to the village and that already she did feel both safe and welcomed.

"I have to agree," said Ty. "I've called it home ever since I was born. Now, I should check in with the king and see if anything has happened. I'd like to suggest that you head to the bakery, where you'll probably find some, if not all, of the teens. It's a popular place to hang out. Enjoy!"

"Thanks, Ty," said Illyra, and Ty left for the village hall.

"So, Chauncey," said Illyra, "do you think we should check out the bakery?"

Do you think they'll have any dog treats?

Illyra laughed and ruffled the fur on the top of his head before saying, "I'm sure they must."

Illyra and Chauncey spent a delightful afternoon getting to know the residents of Dragonwind. They realized that they were beginning to make new friends. That felt really good, especially to Illyra, who had never been allowed, with very few exceptions, to meet others her age.

CHAPTER 7

DREAMS AND RESCUES

Illyra returned to Blossom's cave after dinner to find that Blossom and Sage were happily chatting. Blossom had decided that Sage had had enough excitement for one day, so she'd told Illyra that she would fix dinner for the two of them in the cave. But she'd encouraged Illyra to eat with the villagers. Illyra had been happy to follow through with that plan once she was assured that her mother was doing well, and she had enjoyed the company.

As Illyra entered the main room of the cave, she noticed that her mother was sitting on a small couch and that her rolling chair, which she'd lived in during the day for the past three years, was no longer in sight.

Blossom noticed Illyra's glances around the room and said, "Your mother was able, with a little help from me, to walk from the bedroom out to this room."

"That's wonderful," said Illyra as she ran over to hug her mother.

Sage just beamed and said, "It's a miracle."

"Well, miracle or not," said Blossom, "I think you need to get a good night's sleep."

"I agree," said Illyra. "May I help you to our room?"

"Yes, please," said Sage.

As Illyra helped her mother to stand, Blossom said, "Don't hesitate to let me know if you need anything."

"Thanks for all your help," said Sage.

Once they were in their bedroom, Sage said, "I don't think we've shared a bed since you were a little girl."

"Well," said Illyra, "it's a giant bed, which is a good thing, since we'll be sharing with Chauncey as well."

Sage laughed as the giant dog jumped onto the bed with them.

Soon both women were asleep, as was Chauncey, who was gently snoring. But soon Althea was in all their dreams. "I'm here with you both," she said. "I need your help, and you need to know what is going on."

Sage said, "What do you need us to do?"

"Estrea is not happy with these barons," said Althea. "Did you never wonder why Estrea has all of this planet's magic?"

"I didn't even know that," said Illyra. "You mean the other countries in this world don't have magic? Why?"

"I'd forgotten that. I lived in Mlinred before I came to Estrea to be Fergus's bride in an arranged marriage, and it was only then that my magic awoke," said Sage.

"Very true. It's because of the dragons. The dragons and the land are connected in a symbiotic way. And that relationship has allowed for magic to develop here. But now that the dragons are being threatened, the land is fighting back on their behalf."

Sage said, "How is it doing that?"

"Right now it is raining very, very heavily in the west, and that rain is going to cause a flash flood that will destroy the home of one of the barons. If something isn't done, it will also kill the family, including an innocent nine-year-old girl."

"But what can we do?" asked Illyra.

"You need to tell Oscar and Foster to fly to Baron Malcolm's. If they get there before dawn, they should be able to rescue the family."

Illyra immediately woke up and went to find Blossom. She knocked on Blossom's bedroom door and then entered.

"Blossom," said Illyra. "We need to send Oscar and Foster on a rescue mission right away. Can you call them?"

"Yes," said Blossom without any hesitation. "I'll ask them to come here now, and you can let us all know what's going on."

About ten minutes later, Oscar and Foster arrived at Blossom's. Illyra explained what she and Sage had learned in the dream conference with Althea, and Oscar and Foster looked very concerned.

Foster said, "I know where Baron Malcolm's property is, and while they've never had problems with landslides there before, they are near an area that has had problems, and they are located on a cliff above a river. This could be very bad."

Oscar said, "I know we aren't supposed to leave the Aerie lands, but this is an emergency. We need to leave now."

Blossom said, "I agree. I'll let Sapphire and the king know why you've left, and please, don't get yourselves killed."

"We'll do our best," said Foster.

With that, they took off flying south.

When they had left, Blossom said, "And now we wait. I think it would be sensible to try to sleep until morning. I don't see any need to wake anyone now."

Illyra nodded, and then said, "I sure hope everyone will be OK."

"I doubt that Althea would have warned you if there wasn't a chance for a rescue," said Blossom.

The weather grew much worse as the two dragons flew southwest. It was nearly dawn when they arrived at Baron Malcolm's estate. That's when they saw that the hill behind Malcolm's home was beginning to slide down onto the house. As they watched in horror, mud slid right over the house, taking the house and surrounding trees farther down the hill.

They saw Malcolm and his wife, Miranda, running toward the slide, shouting, "Molly!"

Then they saw a small girl being swept along in the mudslide.

Oscar and Foster immediately flew over to the slide. Oscar flew down and grabbed for the little girl, but she was so muddy that he lost his grip.

Foster came down right behind him and also made a grab for Molly. He managed to grab onto her nightshirt, and he pulled carefully but firmly.

The mud was so viscous that he had a very difficult time trying to pull her free of the landslide. And the landslide was gathering speed.

Malcolm came running over to the dragons and said, "Would this rope help?"

Oscar said, "Yes. Tie it into a large slip knot, and we'll try to get it over her head and around her torso."

The three of them worked at that. Foster held tight until Malcolm had made the slip knot and Oscar was in position to drop it over Molly. When everything was in position, Foster said, "I'll let go just long enough for the rope to go over her. Be quick because I'll need to grab her right back, or else we'll lose her entirely."

"Now," said Oscar as he lowered the rope.

Foster let go for only a second or two, but Oscar was quick, and by the time Foster had grabbed Molly's nightshirt, the rope was around her. Oscar then pulled the rope tightly around her. He had to pull it a lot harder than he wanted to because he couldn't get it under her arms. He was afraid that she might get some rope burns when Foster pulled on the rope, but he figured rope burns were better than drowning in mud.

"OK, Foster," said Oscar when he had the rope as securely fastened around Molly as he could manage.

Foster nodded and then, taking a firm hold on the other end of the rope, Foster began to pull upward and against the flow of the landslide. At first, nothing seemed to be happening. But then, suddenly there was a sick sucking sound. Next, Molly seemed to pop out of the mud like a cork coming out of a bottle. Then she was swinging below Foster, dangling by the rope.

Foster flew higher, away from the landslide, just as Malcolm and Miranda's home slid over a cliff and into the river below. Oscar called to Foster to let him know where it was safe to land, and soon, Foster was lowering Molly to the ground in front of her parents. Miranda got the rope off of Molly as Malcolm wiped off her face and pulled large quantities of mud from her nose and mouth.

For a few moments it looked as if the rescue had been in vain, but Malcolm kept working on his daughter, and after a few minutes, she started coughing and crying. Oscar had been right about the rope burns, and Molly was in shock, but her parents were with her, and the dragons were pretty sure she would be all right.

Foster said, "I think we should fly you all back to Dragonwind, where we have healers who can help. Would that be all right?"

At first, Malcolm and Miranda just stood, uncertainty etched across their faces. They'd been told for so long that dragons were evil, the enemy. But then they looked down at Molly and shook themselves. They'd been fed lies, and they'd believed them. But no more. Suddenly, both Malcolm and Miranda ran over to the two dragons and tried to hug them. They had tears running down their faces and could only nod.

Oscar bent a front leg and said, "Well, then climb onto my back."

Malcolm helped Miranda to climb onto Oscar, and then he lifted Molly up to her. Then he picked up a small chest, asking, "Can I bring this?"

Foster said, "Sure."

So Malcolm awkwardly climbed onto Foster with his chest, and they took off for Dragonwind, the dragons flying as fast as they could. Foster called ahead to Blossom to alert her and also asked her to let Sapphire, the king, Ty, and Criseda all know what had happened.

A little over an hour later, Foster and Oscar were landing on the village green. Martha and Blossom were there, and they immediately got the family into the village hall so that they could be tended to. Martha had already prepared a hot bath for Molly, and it didn't take long to get her into it. Kyle showed Miranda and Malcolm where they could get clean, and he also gave them fresh clothes.

A bed had been made up in one of the sleeping areas for them, and soon Molly was tucked under warm covers, clean from her bath, and with her rope burns treated. Hot food and drinks were also provided.

Finally, Malcolm looked at the king and said, "Sire, I'm so sorry. I believed Fergus and the others. I've never met a dragon before. But Oscar and Foster risked their lives without a moment's hesitation, and if it hadn't been for them, Molly would have died. The rains came down so hard, and somehow

I knew I'd have to get my family out of the house. I grabbed my box of important items and hurried my wife and daughter out of the house. But then my daughter ran back into the house for a favorite toy, and I dropped my box and raced for her. I didn't have time as the house started to be buried in mud. If Oscar and Foster hadn't arrived when they did, she would have been lost. As it is, she came very close, nearly drowning in mud. From now on, I will not support any actions that put any creatures in danger, especially dragons."

Bertram looked at Malcolm for a few moments before he nodded and said, "We'll talk more this weekend, but I do hope no one else has to learn this lesson the way you and your family had to."

"Just rest now," said Ty. "There'll be time for figuring out what's going on once you're recovered."

Ty and Criseda returned to their cave, and Ty pondered this change in the land's dynamics. This was a major development, one that he didn't think had ever happened before, certainly not in his lifetime. He wondered just what the land wanted and how the land's wishes would play into either their plans or the barons' plans.

CHAPTER 8

COUNCIL MEETING

The weekend was fun for both the villagers and their guests. The most popular activity seemed to be dragon rides for everyone, especially the kids. Oscar, Foster, and Criseda gave most of the rides, but Blossom, Sapphire, and Driselda also joined in. Even Bergamen, who tired more easily as a result of this smaller wing, which was augmented by an addition that Raymond had designed, managed to give rides to the smallest children.

Rides on Wilhelmina were nearly as popular as the dragon rides, especially since she could take riders into the forests surrounding the village. Paul was happy to sit behind Ernest for rides on Wilhelmina. He felt very grown up being tasked with keeping the youngest of Bertram and Elicia's family safe.

Sage stayed close to Elicia during the day, and she was noticeably more mobile as the weekend progressed. Miranda joined them, and the three of them could be seen conversing seriously at times.

Illyra felt a bit overwhelmed by all the activities. She realized that she had really lived a very isolated life, and now that her mother was needing less and less help, she wondered how her life would change and what she would do. But soon she was hanging out with the other teens, who seemed determined to include her in all their activities.

Illyra learned all about how each of them had arrived in Dragonwind, what their lives had been like before they arrived, and what they were doing now. After hearing each of their stories, Illyra didn't feel anywhere near as lonely or uncertain.

"So you've all found places to belong?" she asked.

Esme answered and said, "Yes, and the past is just that. It's true that the slum area had been a constant feature for, well, since long before we were born, so it was pretty well ingrained in our society. The king had tried removing greedy money lenders and landlords, but then things would just return to the way they'd always been.

"But now, thanks in large measure to the help of the dragons, the entire area has finally been completely rebuilt. To keep it moving in the right direction, Fen, Jasper, and I are now helping on Queen Elicia's committee to help the residents in the capital find homes and jobs. Lance is also on that committee, and while we've gotten most of the people who had been living in the slum situated with new, better lives, there are still some who need our help."

Fen continued, "And there are a lot of kids who need help with school and encouragement to find their path as well."

"Wow," said Illyra.

Then she turned to Lyra, who said, "I'm still here in Dragonwind, and I'm very happy about that. Martha and Kyle would have had a hard time losing us all at once. Jasper and Esme are also being fostered by them, but now they live most of the time in the palace. But I'm studying to be a vet, and while I'm sure there are animals in the capital, there are many more, especially larger animals like cattle, goats, and sheep, here in Dragonwind, and also over in Rocking Rocks."

Illyra stroked Chauncey's head and said, "And you all have bonded partners?"

"Yes," said Esme, as Rupert, a fox, and Samantha, a squirrel, scooted closer to her.

Lyra gave Matilda, the fox, a hug and said, "We wouldn't feel complete without our partners."

Matilda added, *I'm sure Chauncey feels the same about you.*

Illyra nodded, and she realized just how true that was. She also thought it was pretty nice to find others who were also bonded and who understood just what that meant.

▲

Finally, the weekend was over. After a lovely dinner, King Bertram stood up and addressed the group of villagers and guests.

"Tomorrow afternoon I will be holding a council meeting here," he began. "Ty, Criseda, Esme, Jasper, and Bergamen are already on the council. And the council meetings are also open to any who want to observe. In addition, observers are also permitted a chance after the main agenda to ask questions or make comments. I would specifically ask that Sage and Illyra attend, if that's OK with you both," Bertram said.

Sage said, "Of course, Bertram. And I think Miranda should also be there. I know Malcolm is on your council, but Elicia and I have been talking with Miranda, and we do think that the council could use more input from women."

"That's a great idea," said Bertram. "Anyone else, either villagers or guests, who wants to attend will certainly be welcome."

With that, everyone stood and headed to their respective accommodations.

During the night, Sage and Illyra shared another dream with Althea. They were looking down from the Aerie, where neither woman had yet been, and Althea said, "I'm really glad that you were able to help save Malcolm and his family. That will cut into Fergus's domination, but it won't be enough to accomplish what needs to be done."

Sage said, "What else can we do?"

"If needed, please remind everyone of how the dragons have rescued humans many times over the centuries," said Althea. "This latest rescue is one of the smallest, though it is nonetheless important. But the dragons helped to fight off The Wraith, a truly evil magical force, not once, but twice. And they helped curtail Jasper's father's ambitions. Each time magic has been used to harm others, the dragons have been able to take that magic away. And Sapphire has also stripped the perpetrators' memories, so that there is no need for a prison, and the perpetrators have been able to start down a better path."

Sage and Illyra pondered this information, and finally Illyra said, "Won't the barons say that without the dragons and those with magic, none of this would be needed?"

"And as far as it goes," said Althea, "that is technically true. However, that's where this latest rescue is so important, not just for Malcolm and his family, but for all of Estrea. I told you that magic has developed because of a synergy between the dragons and humans. And this time it triggered a reaction from the land itself. The barons didn't cause that weather anomaly. The land did that all on its own in response to the threat to the dragons and magic in general. And if the likes of Fergus aren't stopped, it will happen again and again. It's becoming very clear that it is the synergy between the land, the dragons, and the humans that has resulted in the presence and development of magic, and all three groups are necessary. Right now, the land seems to be very unhappy."

Sage said, "We'll do our best."

"Thanks," said Althea. "Now sleep well."

With that, the dream ended, and both Sage and Illyra slept deeply for the remainder of the night.

In the morning the village was alive with activity as preparations were made for the council meeting. The cots and sleeping accommodations were moved aside so that a large table could be set at one end of the long rectangular room. Chairs were set up around the table for the council members, with spaces left for the dragons, who didn't need them. Bertram and Elicia would be sitting at the center of one long side, with Ty and Criseda on Bertram's right followed by Fen, Esme, Jasper, and Bergamen on Elicia's left. Malcolm would be next to Bergamen. The other eight barons, including Fergus, would be seated around the remainder of the table.

Martha and Naomi had set up a refreshment table off in the corner behind the conference table. If the barons arrived early enough, they would be given lunch, but if they arrived just in time for the meeting, then they would be able to grab food and beverages to sustain them after their four-hour trek from the capital.

Aloysius and Driselda had a smaller table in the other corner behind the conference table, and they had already assembled a formidable collection of parchments that they could use to provide the necessary documentation for the Aerie boundary changes.

Sapphire had been offered a place at the council table since she was an integral part of the proceedings, but she pointed out that the table should be used only for the actual council and that she would have a front-row spot in the area set up for any who wanted to attend.

Rows of chairs had been set up facing the council table, and a spot in the center of the first row was set up for Sapphire. Next to her spot, there were chairs for Sage and Illyra, as well as Miranda. Martha had agreed to watch Molly, as it was decided that she didn't need to be present unless someone demanded to see her. Finally, Oscar and Foster would be present after they checked each of the barons for any weapons. It was important to have those most affected in the front row so all could see them, and so they could speak up when they wanted.

When all was configured to Bertram's specifications, the group had their lunch. They'd just finished when Fergus and his fellow barons walked into the hall, followed closely by Oscar and Foster. The barons did not look happy.

Bertram welcomed them and asked them to be seated. Once everyone was settled, the king opened the meeting.

"This is an emergency meeting to discuss the concerns about the ancient treaty between humans and dragons," he began.

Fergus interrupted. "There's nothing to discuss. The treaty is valid, and we are not going to overturn it."

"You will have your chance to speak, Fergus," said the king. "First I call on our historian, Aloysius, and the dragons' historian, Driselda." When Fergus started to protest, Bertram held up his hand and said, "The treaty states that the dragons are required to stay within the Aerie boundaries. It is only prudent to have those boundaries defined so all know where they are."

Aloysius and Driselda stood and moved into the center of the space between the council and the audience. Then Aloysius began, "The treaty was very lax in defining the actual boundaries of the Aerie. The terms just say, 'the top of the mountain.' This allows for some expansion, and the villages of Dragonwind and Rocking Rivers have petitioned to leave Estrea and join the Aerie."

"We have all the necessary paperwork here, properly signed, to allow that, and Sapphire has generously agreed to annex the villages," said Driselda, holding up the documents.

Fergus said, "I don't care about a couple of unimportant backwater villages. Now we need to vote."

"Very well," said King Bertram in a weary, discouraged voice. "We will begin with Ty."

Ty said, "I vote to rescind the treaty."

Criseda, Esme, Jasper, and Bergamen also voted for rescinding the treaty. Then the king called on Malcolm, noting the smug look on Fergus's face.

Malcolm reached down under his chair and brought up the small chest he'd brought with him and placed it on the table. Then he stood, keeping his hand on the chest. He said, "Many of you already know that my daughter, Molly, nearly died when a sudden landslide hit our home. But I need to explain to you all just what happened."

"No, you don't," said Fergus. "We don't care. Now just vote."

Malcolm looked to Bertram and said, "May I tell my story?"

"Certainly," said Bertram.

"Thank you," said Malcolm. "You see, Fergus is right that he doesn't care. All he really cares about is money and power, and he'll do anything to keep that. He thinks he commands my vote, as well as the votes of the other seven barons here.

"But he no longer commands my vote. I'll get to that in a moment, but even before the landslide, I was having second thoughts about Fergus's plan to wipe out the dragons and any beings with magical power. He wants to eradicate the changes that King Bertram has brought about. So I quietly sold off my property and possessions and raised enough money to pay back my loan to Fergus. I want you to know about the landslide first. My land was never hit by a landslide before. It isn't in an area that is prone to them, and

I couldn't imagine why we had so much rain or why the land turned into a muddy liquid. I know now that the land itself turned against me."

"That's absurd," yelled Fergus.

"Is it? Your own wife and daughter have explained to Miranda and me exactly what happened that night. You see, they were able to sense the landslide and the danger that my daughter would be in. If it weren't for them, well, I don't even want to think about that. They alerted Oscar and Foster, who, without any hesitation, immediately left the safety of the Aerie and flew to our aid. They were willing to risk their lives to save Molly."

Malcolm then recapped the evening's events in vivid detail before continuing. "Molly is still weak, but she's recovering, and as we gather here, she's outside with Bertram's daughters and youngest son along with the foster orphans who are being cared for here, playing in the sun. A magnificent moose named Wilhelmina is watching over the children so that they are safe while we hold this meeting.

"You, Fergus, want to banish or kill the very beings who have saved me. I now realize how close I was to losing the only point to living. It isn't money or power; it is family and love, and thanks to Sage, Illyra, Oscar, Foster, Ty, Blossom, Martha, and indeed all the fine people of this 'backwater' village, I have all I need."

Malcolm then opened the chest and removed several sacks of coins as well as a piece of parchment. He handed them to King Bertram and said, "I would like you to witness this transaction. The sacks contain every bit of what I owe Fergus, and this parchment is the document with details of the loan. It states clearly that no money is owed unless I fail to vote as Fergus directs. I haven't yet voted, so I am paying back the loan before he can call it in. Fergus needs to sign it as paid in full, and if you and Sapphire can witness that, I will then cast my vote."

Malcolm sat down, and Bertram picked up the parchment, read it, and then handed both it and the sacks over to Fergus.

"You'll regret this, Malcolm," said Fergus. "I'll ruin you."

"I have everything I need," said Malcolm calmly as he looked at his wife.

"Fine," snapped Fergus as he snatched up a pen and signed the parchment. Bertram and Sapphire did the same.

Then Bertram said, "So now, Malcolm, may we have your vote?"

"Yes," said Malcolm. "I vote to rescind the treaty. We cannot live without the dragons and their magic. The land won't allow it."

King Bertram nodded and then turned to Fergus. But just then the door to the village hall opened, and a large delegation of citizens hurried in. Their leader came right up to the table and said, "Sorry we are late. My name is Humphrey, and I'm the leader of the merchant guild in the capital. It took longer to get here than we thought because we were stopped at every village along the route."

King Bertram looked at Humphrey, who was holding a large sheaf of parchments, and said, "You are here now. How can we help you?"

"We're in the middle of a vote," complained Fergus, "and we need to get that done so we can leave for home, as it's a long way."

"I'm aware of that," said the king, "but these people have also come a long way, and what they have to say might influence the vote. We will hear them first."

"B-b-but," stammered Fergus.

The king held up a hand and said, "They will be heard."

As these proceedings were going on, Illyra watched not only her father, who seemed deeply upset at not getting to control the meeting, but also at the other barons. Most of them were doodling or looking bored, but one of them, the man sitting right next to her father, seemed to be doing his best not to be noticed. He was a very ordinary, nondescript man, but he had strange eyes.

Illyra found it difficult to look at him. It was as if her eyes couldn't focus on him. But every once in a while, he would stare at her and her mother. Then she got a glimpse of real hatred and venom in his eyes, as if his true feelings were being revealed. She saw that same hatred when Malcolm was saying how wonderful and good the dragons were.

Illyra decided that this man must be the Zythrym who'd somehow managed to get a copy of the old treaty for her father. She wondered what his stake in all of this was. She felt that he was somehow telling her father what to do, stirring up Fergus's anger and rage.

She turned back to watch the king as he turned to Humphrey and said again, "How can we help you?"

Humphrey said, "We have signed parchments not only from the capital but from every village and town between the capital and here. They all want to secede from Estrea and join the Aerie, if that is agreeable to the dragons."

"What!" shouted Fergus. "You can't."

Humphrey looked down his long nose at Fergus and said, "We already have."

Bertram turned to Aloysius and Driselda and said, "Would you two please take these documents and check them out while we hear from Humphrey?"

Humphrey took his parchments over and placed them on the table where Aloysius and Driselda were and then returned to address the king.

Humphrey began, "All of us here," and he waved to the group of about fifty men and women, "were worried when you began all the changes after the explosions. Many of us don't live in that area or have shops there, but the change just seemed impossible. That area had been a slum area for lifetimes, and change never seemed an option. Even those of us with shops in that area, well, we were just trying to keep our places of business open.

"But then you brought in help. You asked the dragons to take down the buildings that were falling down anyway and to level the ground that had tunnels running underneath it and bomb craters from several explosions. We just watched. But then we saw dancing dragons," he said with a chuckle. "Do you remember that?"

Several in the group nodded, and Humphrey continued. "I'll never forget that sight, nearly twenty dragons dancing and stomping, taking down the derelict buildings and leveling the ground." Turning to look at the dragons, he said, "I hope you still dance. I hope you will always dance. Because you know what you did for us? You gave us the hope that things could actually change, that life could get better for our capital. Many of us had been a bit wary of dragons and magic because we didn't understand it. But there could be no doubt that they were trying to help us.

"So we watched, almost afraid to hope, but we did. And then you, your majesty," said Humphrey, looking at the queen, "you and your committee," he continued looking at Esme, Fen, Jasper, Lance, and Raymond, "you all swept into the area, and you opened up schools; you offered jobs and apprenticeships, you taught people to read, but most of all, you brought the same hope that the dancing dragons had.

"Well, it's a year later now, and we all realized that things have gotten a lot better already. Thanks to not only the king's efforts, but the hard work of the dragons, this time the reforms actually have lasted. Never before was the area razed to the ground and everything rebuilt, solidly and affordably. The slums are gone. The area is well cared for. Very few are still homeless, and most importantly, we know you are still there, helping. You haven't abandoned anyone. The businesses in the entire capital, not just in the former slum area, but everywhere, well, we're doing better, significantly better. And crime is way down.

"The biggest crime before was theft, because people were desperate. But that has nearly disappeared. Life is good." Then Humphrey turned to look at Fergus and the other barons and said, "I have no idea why you would object. I can only think it is because you are no longer profiting from the misery of others. But we are sticking with King Bertram, Queen Elicia, the dragons—if you'll have us, Sapphire—and all those who are interested in the welfare of others.

"I guess that's all I have to say, sire. That and thank you from all of us," concluded Humphrey.

There was an enormous outpouring of applause at that point, although Illyra again noticed Zythrym whispering to her father. When King Bertram was finally able to call the meeting back to order, he said, "Thank you, Humphrey. Does anyone else want to speak while Aloysius and Driselda are conferring?"

A small, timid-looking man at the back of the group raised his hand, and the king nodded to him, saying, "Go ahead."

The man said, "My name is Timothy, and I'm a baker in the former slum area. I wanted to reaffirm all that Humphrey has said, and also to add a personal story."

He looked right at Fen and said, "Fen, I remember the day of the last explosion, an explosion which cost you your mother, who was a wonderful woman. But what I remember most about that day was seeing you earlier when you stopped by my bakery, as you often did. And yes, I know that many times you stole a loaf of bread. I was struck by the fact that it was always a stale loaf, never a fresh one. And that fateful day, you talked to me as you took the loaf, saying that maybe I should consider giving away my stale bread, as I was certainly not making any money off it, but that throwing it out was depriving food to those who were starving. Do you remember that?"

Fen looked a bit embarrassed but nodded.

"That was the beginning of the food pantry that you started," Timothy continued. "You suggested that I ask others to do the same, the green grocers and the butchers. We'd honestly never thought that we could do anything, and you opened our eyes. As you know, I've thanked you personally a number of times since that day, but I wanted to tell it now in front of all these folks, not to embarrass you—well, not much," he chuckled, "but to show how we can all make a difference if we just think about others. You," he said, turning to Fergus, "you have never thought about anyone else. I understand your wife and daughter have left you. What do you have? Nothing important." Then, turning to the king, he said, "Thank you, sire, and you, Queen Elicia. You have given so much to those of us who grew up in the slums. We will always stand with you wherever you are."

"That's heartbreaking, I'm sure," sneered Fergus. "Can we now vote?"

King Bertram looked over at Aloysius and Driselda and asked, "So, what's the verdict?"

Driselda said, "If the request from the capital were the only request, it wouldn't have been valid, because the treaty clearly states that the Aerie has to be a continuous area. I think those drafting it wanted to keep the dragons and their riders from picking other random spots to settle. However," Driselda continued, holding up a front leg to stop the comments from Fergus and his barons, "the fact that Humphrey and his fellow merchants took the time to stop in each village along the way leaves us with a very different picture."

Driselda went over to the map of Estrea that was on the wall and began pointing to all the towns and villages who were requesting to be part of the Aerie, and she said, "As you can see from the map, the Aerie, which was fairly circular, now has become, if we honor the requests, a circle with a long tail leading all the way to the capital. Hence, it meets the treaty requirements."

"What!" shouted Fergus. "That can't be."

Aloysius confirmed, "Oh, but it is. There is no doubt that the Aerie would now run from the north of Estrea right down to the middle."

King Bertram turned to Sapphire with a smile on his face and said, "Sapphire, will you accept these new lands into the Aerie?"

"With the greatest pleasure," she replied, "and we will protect them from any harm."

King Bertram then turned to Fergus and the other barons who hadn't voted yet. Fergus was looking furious, and Zythrym turned to stare at Illyra and Sage with a burning rage in his eyes. He seemed to blame them for this change in allegiances, but Illyra couldn't figure out why he would blame them.

Then the king said, "We can finish the voting now. I just want to make very sure that you recognize the new boundaries of the Aerie, which include everything from here down to and encompassing the capital. By the way, that also includes your home in the capital."

"But not my factories and housing estates to the south," said Fergus. "Yes, let's vote, as we need to go home."

There was no surprise when the other barons sided with Fergus, and the king announced, "The treaty stands with a vote of eight to six against rescinding it. We will adjourn the meeting. I would also like to offer transportation back to the capital for any who would like it. My family and I will be returning in the morning."

Sapphire said, "And for any who are interested, my dragons and I would like to offer rides to any of you who would like them, as our way of saying thank you to you for all your loyalty and support. We could have you there in about an hour. Just let Ty know if you would like that either now or tomorrow, and we'll arrange it."

As everyone stood, Fergus stormed over to Sage, who had Star on her shoulder, and Illyra, with Chauncey beside her, and said, "I'm not done with the two of you yet."

"Too bad," said Sage, "as we are done with you. I'm divorcing you, and in fact, I believe Aloysius is just coming to serve you with the divorce papers, which both King Bertram and Sapphire have signed."

"And I'm now of age," said Illyra. "You are no longer my guardian."

Fergus looked at the two of them and just seemed to realize that Sage was standing. "You-you-you're not paralyzed," he stammered.

"No," said Sage. "Ty and Blossom have healed me. Seems your influence isn't as great as you thought. I think Malcolm said it best when he said that he had all he needed. The same is true for us. We neither need nor want you."

"You'll regret this," said Fergus as he stormed out of the hall, snatching the papers out of Aloysius's hand.

Malcolm and Miranda came over and said, "So are you OK?"

Sage said, "Definitely. It was quite a meeting."

CHAPTER 9

DEPARTURES

Everyone moved out onto the village green to decide who was leaving, when, and how. Ty called to everyone and said, "Those of you who would like to take the dragons up on their offer of transport, please step over here." Ty pointed to a spot on the green, and people began to move.

When Fergus and a couple of the barons moved to the spot, Ty said, "Really? Are you planning to change your votes?"

"No," snapped Fergus.

"Well, the dragons are doing this as a way to thank those who supported them," said Ty. "You can find your own way back."

"What?" said Fergus. "They're just animals. I'd be happy to hire them."

Ty shook his head and said, "They are intelligent creatures, obviously more intelligent than you are. Please leave Dragonwind immediately."

"You can't deny me a ride," said Fergus.

Sapphire strolled over and said, "No dragon will ever help you in any way, not after all you have done. Do I make myself clear?"

Fergus frowned and thought about Sapphire's words. He couldn't believe how she was thwarting him. Nobody ever did that without consequences. He wouldn't allow it. Today hadn't been a good day. First he'd had to come to this backwater village. Then Malcolm had defied him. That was something else that had never happened before. At least the vote had gone his way. He'd have to be sure to wipe out all the dragons before Bertram could do something else to change things. Once he had that done, then he'd get rid of all the do-gooders who were changing the capital. He needed things to go back to what they'd been before. He'd show them.

Just then Sage and Illyra walked over. Fergus looked at them and then said, "Are you coming with me?"

Sage let out a loud laugh and said, "You really are the stupidest, most self-centered narcissist that ever lived."

Illyra, keeping her hand on Chauncey, said, "I am so glad that I will never have to deal with you again."

"You will marry whomever I say," said Fergus. "It's the only way you will be safe from an even worse fate."

Fergus couldn't believe that these weak women were actually defying him. Today was definitely not going his way, but he had plans in place that would change everything.

"Delusional, isn't he?" said Ty. "Now get out of here. If you are still in the village when I check in ten minutes, then you will get a ride with a dragon, dangling from their claws and getting thrown over the nearest cliff."

Finally, this had the desired effect, and Fergus hurried off, followed by his fellow barons, shouting, "You will regret this, Bertram."

Fergus and his group headed out of the village and into the woods. Zythrym pulled Fergus aside and said, "So are your men ready, as I asked?"

"Yes, yes," said Fergus. "You described the geography of the Aerie perfectly, and we'll be able to destroy a large area. I can't believe that I have to go through this again. My family forced the dragons onto that horrible land centuries ago. The treaty was well drafted. But now we're having to fight it out all over again."

"Don't worry," said Zythrym. "You'll prevail."

No one noticed that as Fergus and his men moved up the path to the Aerie to meet up with others, Zythrym wasn't with them. He'd just vanished.

▲

Once the barons were gone, Ty looked at those who'd indicated that they would like a dragon ride back to the capital. He said, "OK, now can you let me know if you want to go back tonight or if you'd like to wait until morning? We can provide accommodations for you if you wish to stay overnight."

The group whispered among themselves before saying, "We would like to go tonight. We've left our families and businesses, and we need to get back to them."

Sapphire said, "We'll be happy to take you tonight. Each dragon will be able to take two at a time, three, even, if you are small. It all depends on weight. Can you sort yourselves into groups?"

As they were doing that, a group of over twenty dragons landed in the village. Soon the groups were sorted, and the dragons began taking off, heading to the capital. Ty said, "Feel free to fly over Fergus and the barons."

"We will," said Oscar, who had volunteered to help transport the merchants.

Once the merchants were gone, Ty went over to Sage and Illyra. "What about you two? Do you know what you want to do now?"

Sage spoke first, saying, "Elicia has invited me to stay at the palace and to join her task force. We are quite sure that I'm not the only wife who's been abused. I'd really like to help other wives break away from unhappy and unhealthy situations."

"That sounds like an excellent goal," Ty said. "What about you, Illyra?"

Illyra rubbed Chauncey's head before saying, "I'm really not sure. I'd love to see the Aerie proper, where Sapphire and the others live. And I'd like to work with Driselda to share my great-grandmother's thoughts and ideas."

"I'm sure you would be most welcome, and a tour would be easy to arrange," said Ty. "We could do it tomorrow after those who are returning to the capital leave."

"Thanks."

"And Sage, I'd be happy to work some more on your back before you leave," said Ty. "I can tell you're moving much more easily, but don't overdo it. Your muscles aren't used to being used."

"I just had to be sure that Fergus saw me walking," she said with a grin, "but you are right; I am getting tired."

"I'll help you get back to Blossom's cave," said Illyra,

"And I can stop by in about an hour," agreed Ty. "I want to touch base with King Bertram first."

Sage nodded, and she and Illyra headed back to Blossom's just as Jeb came running up to Ty. Illyra heard Jeb say, "There are a bunch of Fergus's men on the path to the Aerie, just out of Dragonwind's borders. Kyle and I have been watching them, but we're worried now because Fergus and his group of barons have just joined them. Kyle is following them now."

Ty said, "That doesn't sound good. We'd better check on them."

Suddenly, there was a very large explosion. The two men headed for the path to the Aerie, just as Illyra let out a cry and started running toward the path. Chauncey howled as he raced after her, and Star also flew toward the Aerie. Sage cried out, "The dragons are in danger. Help!"

Ty looked around and saw Sage crumple to the ground. But he also saw Martha and Naomi hurrying toward her to help her. Knowing that Sage would be well cared for, he and Jeb took off up the path at a run. Never had he felt so alone. Criseda was carrying merchants to the city, but he called out telepathically to her anyway. *There's been an explosion at the Aerie.*

Criseda answered immediately. *I know. Sapphire and Driselda are there. Oscar, Foster, and I are landing in a small village right now. We'll leave our passengers there and come back right away.*

Ty felt better as he and Jeb ran as fast as they could toward the Aerie. Illyra and Chauncey were ahead of them, moving faster than Ty thought possible. They could now see Fergus and the others meeting up with a large group of workers. Star was visible just above the group. Ty had never communicated with the raven, but he received a message from her now.

Ty, I will let you hear what the men are saying: Fergus shouted, "Were you successful?" The leader of the workers said, "Yes, we've blown a giant hole in the Aerie. There were only a couple dragons there, just as you said. But there's rubble everywhere." Fergus said, "Excellent. We'll hunt the two that are there and then stay in wait for the others. This is our day."

Star then flew toward Ty as Fergus and all the others headed toward the Aerie. Star landed on Ty's shoulder long enough for her to say, *I've let Sapphire and Driselda know as well. Now I need to go back to Sage. She needs me.*

Ty nodded and said, "Thank you!"

As Star flew back to Dragonwind, Kyle joined Ty and Fergus. He said, "Here, I have bows and arrows for you both."

"Thanks," said Jeb as he took his.

Then the three of them followed after the men. Ty called out telepathically to Sapphire and Driselda. *Kyle, Jeb, and I are on our way. And so are Illyra and Chauncey, although I don't know why. Criseda, Oscar, and Foster have turned around and are headed back.*

Thanks, said Sapphire. *They won't find us to be easy targets, and we will have some surprises for these thugs. "Stupid animals, pack animals"—well they will learn just how wrong they are.*

Ty, Jeb, and Kyle were closing on Fergus's men, but they were careful to stay out of sight. The men didn't seem to sense anything wrong. They just kept moving forward, and soon Ty saw the destruction.

The Aerie had started out as a mountain top that wasn't very large or flat. The dragons, with the help of their riders, had long ago cut the top of the mountain down to form a very large flat surface. They'd turned it into a field for their livestock, and they'd carved out caves for the dragons. The dragons were very careful never to raid human farms for food.

But now, Ty saw the bodies of goats, sheep, and cows, some of them in many pieces, strewn over the land. The land was no longer flat, but instead there was a mammoth crater where the flat fields had been.

Ty heard Fergus say, "Fantastic job!"

Just then Sapphire and Driselda flew up from inside the crater, shooting fire above the men. They were careful not to kill or harm any of the men. They only wanted to scare them and protect the Aerie. When the men hastily backed up and drew out their bows, firing their arrows at the dragons, the two dragons had no trouble burning the arrows or knocking them down. Whenever a man went to reload, Sapphire or Driselda would pick him up and drop him into the crater, a drop of about ten feet.

Finally, when the last man was dropped into the crater, Ty, Kyle, and Jeb came up to stand by Sapphire and Driselda, being careful to stay away from the edge so the few who still had intact arrows and bows and were uninjured enough to use them couldn't get a shot at them.

Criseda, Oscar, and Foster arrived then, and they all stared at the destruction. Finally, once the men were out of arrows, Ty looked down at Fergus and said, "Your actions were illegal even before the Aerie was extended. What did you think you were doing?"

Fergus chuckled and then said, "We didn't actually kill or even harm any dragons, so we didn't violate the treaty. Now get us out of here."

Just then Illyra and Chauncey ran over to Ty and Sapphire. Both of them tried to talk at once. Chauncey said, *There is a hurt dragon here*, just as Illyra said, "I heard cries of pain. Fryzal is trapped in that rubble."

As Ty said, "Who's Fryzal?" Sapphire looked around the debris. Everyone was very quiet, and suddenly all the dragons moved to the largest pile of rubble and began digging. Ty, Kyle, and Jeb, along with Chauncey, moved to help. Then they all heard a small voice whimpering just as Illyra gasped out, "Fryzal is caught and injured."

Sapphire looked alarmed as she said, "Fryzal? But she shouldn't even be here."

Illyra was bending over, grabbing her side to catch her breath, as she said, "She left the nursery so she could see me. It's all my fault."

The dragons were lifting blocks of stone very carefully from the large pile where the whimpering seemed to be coming from. *Any luck?* said a voice behind Ty.

Ty looked to see Wilhelmina behind him, carrying Paul, Sage, and Lyra. Matilda, the fox bonded with Lyra, was standing next to Wilhelmina.

Ty said, "Not so far," as Paul, Sage, and Lyra slid off Wilhelmina's back.

Everyone kept working, making sure that the removal of a stone didn't cause others to fall. It took over half an hour to reach the point where they could see an opening between rocks, and there, shivering in pain, was Fryzal.

Illyra leapt forward and, not even realizing what she was doing, raised her hand and moved the last of the boulders away with telekinetic magic. She gently reached for Fryzal. Lyra watched as Illyra worked to lift the small dragon out of the hole. The little dragon seemed to be changing colors as Illyra brought her out.

Illyra said, "She's gorgeous, but what's wrong with her wing and her left leg?"

Lyra said, "They both appear to be broken. I really can't work on her here. Can we get her back to Dragonwind?"

Sapphire said, "Illyra, can you get up on my back?"

Sapphire bent her front leg to make a step, and with Ty helping to balance her, Illyra, holding Fryzal gently in her hands, managed to get on Sapphire's back.

Then Sapphire said, "Lyra, I think it would help to steady Illyra if you got on behind her."

Ty helped Lyra to get up behind Illyra. When they were settled, Sapphire took off for Dragonwind. As she flew the short distance, she asked Illyra, "Did you know you had telekinetic powers?"

"What?" said Illyra, "Me? No. I just have telepathy but no other magical powers. Why?"

Sapphire chuckled and said, "Well, I think you've just awakened another magical power. The last of the rocks that trapped Fryzal just flew off her when you raised your arm."

Lyra said, "They sure did. It was amazing."

Illyra said, "Really? I had no idea. But what about Fryzal? She's so hurt."

As they landed on the green in Dragonwind, Lyra said, "We'll see to her. I promise."

▲

Once Sapphire and the others had left, Ty looked into the hole and said, "Now don't go anywhere, Fergus. It seems that the situation has changed. You have severely wounded a dragon. You better hope that Fryzal makes it, because if she dies, your life and the lives of your men are forfeit."

"What!" shouted Fergus.

"The terms of the treaty are very clear," said Ty. "You were obviously more interested in how you could kill dragons and riders and totally ignored the consequences of coming onto dragon land and causing damage."

"But that's only one dragon, and there are over twenty of us," said Fergus. "You can't kill that many humans over one small dragon."

"The treaty says differently," said Ty, "and you are so big on following the law. We will hold you to it."

Ty turned to leave, and Fergus called out, "Hey, you need to get us out of here."

Ty looked back at the captives and said, "I think this is a fine prison for you until we know more. I'll be back later."

With that Ty, Jeb, Kyle, and Sage moved away, and Criseda, Oscar, and Foster offered to take them all to Dragonwind. Paul and Wilhelmina said they'd walk back since the dragons couldn't carry a giant moose. As they all left, they could hear the barons and workers shrieking after them.

When they landed on the village green, Martha came out of her home to say, "Lyra is working on poor Fryzal on my kitchen table. She has many injuries and is in a lot of pain."

Sage said, "Illyra heard Fryzal calling telepathically to her from the Aerie, and then she felt Fryzal's pain when the explosion hit. That's what caused her to run to the Aerie. She wouldn't wait. She was beside herself. Paul immediately said that Wilhelmina could take the rest of us, since Illyra was already off and running."

"I understand," said Ty. "It sounds as if Fryzal has already bonded with Illyra, even though they hadn't seen each other. I truly hope Fryzal will be OK."

Sage pondered the significance of this newly formed bond. It would no doubt be transformative for Illyra to be bonded with a dragon, as this would make her links to the dragon community even more profound. Sage hoped the little dragon would be OK, as it would be wonderful for Illyra to have another bonded partner.

CHAPTER 10

CONSEQUENCES

Lyra worked for well over an hour to stabilize Fryzal. The poor little dragon had really been badly damaged when she was caught in the explosion. Blossom helped Lyra by checking all the alignments as Lyra splinted the broken wing and leg. Martha had fixed one of her herbal pain medications, which Lyra then administered. Ty added his own healing magic both to calm Fryzal and to speed the rate of her healing.

Finally, there was no more that could be done. Illyra gently picked up Fryzal and asked if it was OK to take her to Blossom's cave. Lyra said, "Yes, but watch her carefully. If you sense any change, no matter how small, let me know."

"I promise," said Illyra, cradling Fryzal. She and Chauncey then walked back to Blossom's cave. She found a large, soft pillow, which she brought into the guest room and put on the bed before she carefully put Fryzal on the pillow. Then she hunted around the cave and found a small blanket, which she wrapped around her to help support the little dragon.

Finally, Illyra spoke gently to Fryzal. "I won't leave you. We are together now. Chauncey is here as well, and he also will protect you. You are safe."

Sapphire, Ty, and Criseda sat at Martha's and discussed what Fergus and his men had done. Ty said, "Well, Lyra's done a good job of patching Fryzal up, and hopefully she'll live. But the damage from the explosion is extensive. I think I should try to contact Bertram and let him know what has happened. He will have to decide what punishment to inflict."

Sapphire said, "Actually, the punishment decision should be mine, as it is definitely dragon land and property that has been destroyed. According to the treaty that Fergus is so determined to uphold, once we moved to the Aerie, we became responsible for managing our own affairs, without any assistance from Estrea. And the government of Estrea would have no obligations toward us; we'd be left on our own."

"Oh, yes, of course," said Ty. "Well, what do you think?"

"I think they should have to make restitution," said Sapphire. "I expect them to fill the bomb crater, reseed it, and then replace all the livestock they killed."

"That sounds fair," said Criseda. "Fergus won't be happy, but personally, I think that he's getting off easy. Of course, if anything happens to Fryzal, it will be different, but for the moment they can start fixing things."

"I think I should let Bertram know what's happened and what your decision is," said Ty. "Also, do you want to keep them as prisoners in the Aerie? And where will you get all the soil to fill the crater?"

Sapphire thought again about the damage. She seemed to sag as she said, "You know that when humans turned on us, we accepted the worst piece of land in all Estrea. It was rocky and totally devoid of any life. No one wanted it, so they gave it to us. We reworked and rebuilt it. With the help of our riders, we made it home, made ourselves self-sufficient. We made a good life and kept away from humans.

"When events made it untenable for us to stay isolated, we did our best to help all life, to unify Estrea. But apparently things haven't changed as much as I thought. We are still hated, and now our home has been destroyed. Honestly, I don't know if it can be repaired."

It was the first time that Ty had ever heard Sapphire sound discouraged or beaten. He hadn't thought that anything could bring her down, but now he wasn't so sure. But it was Martha who said, "I know you are hurting.

However, do you remember what Timothy said at the meeting, about all the hope that the dragons have given them? And what about all the villages and towns, as well as the capital, who have voted to side with you and King Bertram? I don't know how it was when people turned on the dragons centuries ago, but I had the idea that it was pretty much everyone except for a few dragon riders. I think it is the opposite now. It seems to me that much if not most of Estrea is in favor of the dragons and that they really appreciate all the help that you have offered to all beings.

"Fergus and his crew are the exception not the rule. And yes, they have caused a lot of damage. But we are not going to cave in to this small group. I think that once others hear what has happened, you will find lots of folks ready to help you rebuild."

Sapphire looked around the kitchen and slowly nodded. Then she said, "Thank you, Martha. Sorry; I felt like giving up."

Criseda said, "It has been a tremendous blow for all of us. And losing our home is a vicious blow from a horrible man. But we will rebuild. Remember how Raymond designed a plan to change the old derelict mining town into the vibrant village of Rocking Rocks? Maybe he'd be willing to share ideas about the Aerie. What do you think?"

Ty said, "I think that's a great idea. Why don't Criseda and I fly to the capital and let Bertram know what's happened? We can then ask if Raymond is willing to lend his expertise as an engineer to come up with solutions for you. Would you like that, Sapphire?"

A tear dropped from one of Sapphire's eyes, and after a moment, she said, "Thank you, my dear friends, and please forgive me for my momentary weakness. Yes, Ty, I would like you to take this news to Bertram and see if he has any suggestions for Fergus and his men. And if Raymond is willing to come to survey the damage and offer suggestions, I would be most grateful."

Ty smiled and said, "I suspect once word gets out that the dragons need help, you'll have more offers of help than you can handle. Before the rebuilding of the slum area, many residents in Estrea were afraid of both dragons and magic. I think Fergus is counting on that to still be true. However, as the meeting showed today, that's no longer the case, and as Martha said, most folks are grateful for all the help they have received, both from the dragons and from those of us with magic. The tide has turned, and Fergus and his ilk are on the wrong side. We'll be back as soon as we can. Let's go, Criseda."

As Ty and Criseda took off, Martha said, "I'd like to go check on Fryzal. Would you like to come with me?"

"Definitely," said Sapphire. "And maybe Jasper and Bergamen would like to come as well. I'm sure Bergamen can offer sympathy on the broken wing."

Martha called out, "Jasper, Bergamen, can you come here?"

The two of them came running, saying, "What do you need, Martha?"

"Have you heard of Fryzal's rescue?" said Martha.

"No," said Bergamen. "What's happened to little Fryzal?"

"So you know her?" asked Sapphire, who was Bergamen's grandmother.

"Sure," said Jasper. "We do visit the dragon nursery. That's about the only place that Bergamen can find dragons who are smaller than him."

"Hey," said Bergamen. "I'm not small."

"Of course not," said Jasper, smiling at Bergamen. "What's happened to Fryzal?"

Sapphire quickly brought them up to date on the explosion, the destruction of the Aerie's fields and livestock, and the injuries to Fryzal.

"That's horrible," said Bergamen. "Will she be all right?"

Martha said, "Lyra and Blossom think so, but we thought we'd go check on her and see how she and Illyra are managing. Do you want to come?"

"Yes," said Bergamen.

"For sure," said Jasper.

With that, Sapphire, Martha, Bergamen, and Jasper headed across the village green and onward to Blossom's cave. As they walked, they were pleased to notice that village activities were looking very normal, with kids playing on the green and parents chatting. No one seemed concerned about the earlier explosion. When they arrived, they found Blossom and Sage in the main room. They led the group to the guest room, where they saw that Illyra was on the bed, curled around Fryzal, who was on a pillow. Then Chauncey was curled around both Illyra and Fryzal. All three of them were fast asleep.

Quietly, the group left and went back to the living room. Sapphire then said, "Well, if that wasn't the loveliest sight. Those three will do very well together."

Martha handed a vial of medicine to Sage and said, "If Fryzal needs more help with her pain, she can have three drops of this every hour as needed."

Sage took the vial and said, "Thanks, Martha. I'll let Illyra know when the three of them wake."

Sapphire said, "Well, keep me posted, and Blossom, if Fryzal needs anything, anything at all, let me know right away."

Blossom assured her that she would.

Then Sapphire said, "Well, I'm going back up to the Aerie to try to take stock of things. Martha, could you make up a bag of sandwiches for our prisoners? I can't bear to feed them any of our now very limited supplies. I hate to impose, but. . ."

Martha put a hand on Sapphire and said, "I'll be happy to help."

Jasper said, "Bergamen and I would like to come up to the Aerie to see if we can help. We can bring Martha's sandwiches for you."

Sapphire said, "Thanks! I'll see you two shortly, then."

As Sapphire took off for the Aerie, Jasper and Bergamen followed Martha. Jasper said, "I'll help make those sandwiches, Martha."

Once the sandwiches were made, Martha handed a large bag to him. Jasper and Bergamen then took off for the Aerie.

Once Jasper and Bergamen arrived at the Aerie, they handed the bag over to Sapphire, who took it and then tossed it down into the crater, saying, "Sandwiches for you. That's all you get until tomorrow, so make them last."

Fergus called out. "You can't keep us here."

"Just watch me," said Sapphire. Then she walked away as Fergus began shouting.

Bergamen and Jasper looked at the destruction. "This is horrible," said Jasper.

"How do we come back from this?" asked Bergamen.

"At the moment," said Sapphire, "I'm not sure. But come back we will. None of us is a quitter."

Dragons were returning to the Aerie after taking the merchants to the capital. They were all shocked by what had happened in their absence, and Bergamen wasn't the only one asking, "What now?"

When all the dragons had landed, Sapphire said, "Fergus and his cowardly men took advantage of the fact that most of you were off helping the merchants. But they will find that we are not going to be beaten. We will not be cowed as we once were when humans turned against us."

She looked around the group of over thirty dragons, who nodded in agreement, before she said, "There was only one injury." She then proceeded to tell them how Fryzal, in her eagerness to reach Illyra, had left the nursery and then been caught in the explosion.

There were gasps of horror, as Fryzal was well loved. Sapphire continued, "I've asked Ty to see if Raymond would be willing to come and advise us about the best way to rebuild. And if any of you have ideas, be sure to let me know. But first, we need to clean up the bomb site. I would suggest that gathering all the carcasses for a bonfire would be a good place to start."

Jasper and Bergamen pitched in to help. The pile of carcasses grew throughout the afternoon. Jasper said, "It's horrible that all these animals were just killed for no reason."

"I don't know what the dragons will do," said Bergamen, "now that their herds are gone."

Sapphire said, "We'll have to buy our meat until we can reestablish our herds. We will not steal."

By the time the area was cleaned up, the pile of dead animals was enormous. Sapphire looked at the dragons as she said, "Let's burn this."

The dragons encircled the pile and shot fire at it from all directions. Soon the pyre was hotly burning. The dragons kept the fire going until early evening, by which time everything was ash. At that point Sapphire looked down into the pit at the men and said with heavy sarcasm, "We're done here for now. Have a pleasant evening."

Fergus shouted back, "We need more food."

"Maybe in the morning," said Sapphire as she and the others turned away and headed to their caves.

Bergamen and Jasper decided to head back to Dragonwind. As they went, Bergamen said, "That was horrible. But it could have been much worse. It was only the flat field that was destroyed. All the caves are still intact. And the nursery with all the young ones is safe."

Jasper nodded and added, "As well as Driselda's library of dragon records."

Bergamen agreed, "It would have been quite a tragedy if those had been lost."

When they reached the village green, Jasper said, "Let's stop at Blossom's and see how Fryzal is."

Bergamen nodded and said, "Good idea."

They walked into Blossom's cave and found Lyra, Blossom, Martha, and Sage in the main room. Bergamen said, "How's Fryzal?"

"Sleeping," said Lyra.

"The three of them are still sleeping curled up together as they were before," confirmed Sage.

"Well, I guess that's the best thing Fryzal can do," said Bergamen.

"Yes," said Lyra. She stood and turned to Blossom. "I'm leaving now, but don't hesitate to call me if you need me."

Martha also stood, saying, "I hope they sleep through the night."

Bergamen and Jasper took a quick peek into the guest bedroom before they, too, left. Blossom said, "You are welcome to sleep in here, if you want. I suspect you don't want to take a chance on disturbing them."

"Thanks," said Sage. "I'm suspecting that Althea has something to do with this, so no, I don't want to disturb them."

"I agree," said Blossom. "See you in the morning."

CHAPTER 11

DREAMTIME

Sage and Blossom were correct in their guess. As Chauncey, Illyra, and Fryzal slept, Althea wrapped them all in a dream covering the years right after the humans banished the dragons and riders to the Aerie three centuries ago. They saw firsthand how hurt the dragons and the few humans who accompanied them were. They also saw just how barren and desolate the Aerie was.

Then Althea began to tell them the history of this time period. When the dragons were first banished, there was no magic in the land. Magic came as the land itself reacted to the dragons' banishment. The land was influenced by the synergy between the dragons and those humans who loved them. Each dragon found comfort from a specific human, resulting in the first bondings. Then the pairs developed telepathy, as the dragons refused to use human speech.

When the precursors of the dragons, the Ribendi, had first arrived in Estrea, they had worked diligently to learn the human language so they could communicate with them. But after the banishment, the newly evolved dragons decided that they wouldn't use human speech. They saw no need to communicate with most humans.

But they did want to be able to communicate with their bonded partners. Soon they discovered that magic was developing. The dragons and riders tried to make the Aerie inhabitable, and when they wished for caves to live in, caves appeared. When they wished for some arable land, they soon had it. In the same way, they developed telepathy. Althea said that the dragons thought that they might be the source of the magic, but she had learned over the centuries that the source was actually the land itself.

However, magic only developed in Estrea because that's where the dragons were, so while the magic came from the land, it came because of the love dragons and riders had for each other, from the strength of the bonds between the two species. And, of course, the dragons came from the Ribendi, who only stayed in Estrea instead of continuing on their explorations because they found some bonding of their own with the land itself and saw a greater potential for Estrea. Ultimately, as the Ribendi brought forth the dragons, it was the triad of the land, the dragons, and their riders that brought forth magic. As time went on, and bonds were broken by the death of one or both parties, the magic reached a stasis. It didn't disappear, but it also didn't grow. This was partly because with the development of magic, a division had arisen within the riders. One rider had decided that this magic could be used to conquer and destroy. He tried first to take over as the leader of the Aerie. When that failed, he began killing both dragons and riders in his bid for power. His own dragon turned on him, and so he was finally banished. "I remember it all too well," said Althea, "and unfortunately, merely banishing him didn't solve the issue. That's one reason I was allowed to dream walk with my descendants. More about that later."

Althea continued. But once he was banished, there was no more growth of magic. Instead, the only humans with magic were those who were descended from those initial riders, although the magic frequently skipped one or more generations. The land stayed quiet unless magic was being used to harm or corrupt. When that happened, the land would bring forth a new form of magic. In the current time, Althea pointed out Ty with his healing magic, then Esme with her ability to read the intentions of others, Windsong and her ability to look into the future, Jasper's telekinesis, and now Illyra and Sage's ability to dream walk, as well as Illyra's newly found telekinesis.

Althea reminded them that dragons had stopped bonding generations ago, but then Windsong had said that the practice needed to return and that dragons also needed to return to working with humans. Jasper and Bergamen were the first of the new bonds, followed closely by Ty and Criseda, and now Illyra and Fryzal. The land's reaction to Fergus's attempts to wipe out magic and dragons was proof that they needed both. Malcolm's experience was going to be repeated again and again if those like Fergus weren't stopped.

Chauncey, Illyra, and Fryzal absorbed all that Althea needed to teach them. The three of them slept around the clock, not waking until late in the morning of the next day, by which time Ty and Criseda had returned to Dragonwind, along with Oscar and Foster, who brought King Bertram and Raymond.

Ty came immediately to Blossom's cave to check on Fryzal. Lyra was there as well when the three sleepers awoke. Ty and Lyra checked on Fryzal and were amazed to find her to be much better, healing faster than even Ty's magic could accomplish.

"How is this possible?" asked Ty.

Star spoke from Sage's shoulder. "Dream magic."

Ty looked puzzled, but Illyra nodded and said, "Yes, Star is correct. We've shared a dream where Althea told us how magic came to be and why magic is increasing now, according to need." With help from Chauncey and Fryzal, Illyra explained all that they had learned.

"That makes a lot of sense," said Ty. "You'll have to share this with Sapphire and Driselda."

Illyra nodded. Then she said, "Can we go to the Aerie? We need to explain things about the rebuilding of the Aerie. We have information you all will want."

Ty and Lyra looked at Fryzal before Lyra said, "You can't try to fly, Fryzal, and you have to let Illyra carry you. Your leg and wing need more time to heal. Do you promise?"

Fryzal cuddled farther into Illyra's arms and said, "I promise."

Lyra looked at Ty and said, "And I want you to continue using your healing magic on Fryzal."

"Of course," agreed Ty.

"Then let's go," said Illyra.

▲

It took about an hour to get everyone gathered who wanted to go to the Aerie. It seemed as if the villagers wanted to be sure that they were included, as they really wanted to help. Oscar and Foster each carried two riders, while Ty and Criseda took Illyra, Chauncey, and Fryzal. And Wilhelmina took four riders on her back. She wasn't quite as fast as the dragons, but she made the trip much easier than hiking would have been.

By the time they all got to the Aerie, it was quite a group. Sapphire was standing over the pit that contained the prisoners. King Bertram and Raymond looked around at the destruction in horror. "I'm so sorry," said King Bertram.

Sapphire looked over at him and said, "I'm not sure what to do next."

Ty said, "I think you want to hear from Illyra, Chauncey, and Fryzal."

Sapphire looked very surprised but turned to see the new arrivals. She looked first at Fryzal and said, "How are you feeling?"

Fryzal said, "I found Illyra and Chauncey, and we're going to stick together."

Sapphire smiled and said, "That's good. You're in very good hands."

Illyra said, "The three of us had the most amazing dream." She then proceeded to tell everyone about the history that Althea had taught them, concluding, "So you see, the Aerie was actually formed by the land itself. The land felt what was needed, and while the dragons and riders thought they were changing things, the actual changes were done by the power of the land."

Sapphire was speechless for the longest time. Finally she said, "So our magic came from the bonded relationships, not from the dragons alone."

"Yes," said Illyra. "And Althea said that the same thing would happen now. We've already seen what the land did to Malcolm's home. Well, the land will also give you the power to repair the Aerie. However, Althea said that you were going to get a lot of offers of help, and if you look at all those who insisted on coming here now, you can see just how true that is. Althea said it was that help that would enhance the magic and that you will learn a lot from accepting all the help that you are about to be surrounded by."

Sapphire looked around her and then down at the pit before she said, "I think I'm already seeing it. This pit isn't as deep this morning as it was last night."

"What?" said Ty.

"It's also reshaping itself," said Sapphire. "I'd heard that magic was involved in the original building of the Aerie, but somehow I assumed that was the dragons' doing. However, it seems from both what I'm observing and what Althea told you that it wasn't the dragons at all."

Jeb and Kyle rode up then, leading a string of horses behind them. Jeb dismounted and said, "We found where Fergus and his men were camping. We not only found their horses and camping supplies but we also found the bags of money that Malcolm had paid Fergus."

Fergus, who had been listening from the pit, shouted up, "Hey, that's mine."

King Bertram looked at Sapphire, who said, "I'd be very happy if you took these villains off my hands. I know the damage has been done to the Aerie, but they are humans—maybe sad excuses for humans, but still yours."

King Bertram nodded and said, "I understand. Let's get them out of there and then tie them up."

Kyle and Jeb made short work of Fergus and his men. They were cold and tired. Several of them had minor injuries, and a couple had badly broken legs, a result of falling into the pit. Once they were secured, Bertram said, "You have caused major damage to the Aerie and nearly killed an infant dragon. At the very least, you owe compensation for the damage. This money, and all your horses and camping supplies, are now Sapphire's."

"What!" yelled Fergus. "You can't do that."

King Bertram smiled and said, "I believe I just did that. Jeb, Kyle, can you get the horses and supplies down to the capital and sell them? I believe they'll fetch a larger price there."

"That's what we thought," said Kyle. "I also thought we could accept store credit instead of actual cash, as it looks as if there will be lots of things the dragons need."

Sapphire said, "I would appreciate that, and our biggest need will be livestock, if that helps you to decide where to negotiate on our behalf."

Jeb nodded, and he and Kyle left to take the horses to the capital.

King Bertram then looked at Oscar and Foster and said, "Any ideas about getting this crew to Simion and the palace guard?"

Foster looked at Sapphire and asked, "Could we have some help for that?"

Sapphire smiled and said, "I believe that if you ask for volunteers, you'll get plenty of takers."

Sapphire was correct. No sooner had she spoken when six dragons volunteered. They picked up the men, one in each front claw, and carried them dangling below their bellies. These guys were not going to ride on their backs. As the dragons took off, the men shouted in terror. Foster said, "This will be an educational experience for them."

Oscar was carrying Fergus, and as they flew, Oscar could read Fergus's thoughts. Fergus kept replaying all that had happened to him. He couldn't believe that Malcolm had stopped following him. And how had Malcolm managed to save enough to repay his debt?

Nothing had gone right since the dragons helped King Bertram remake the old slums. Before that, things had been the same for decades. The proper order of things had been maintained, with the wealthy taking advantage of the poor, as they got wealthier and more powerful. That was how things were supposed to be.

It was all the work of the dragons that was bringing down the established order of society, and everything he'd tried so far had failed. But not for long! Fergus had more plans that even his closest advisors, including Zythrym, knew nothing about. After all, he was meant to be in charge. He was meant to take control from the weak. That's what his ancestors had done when they wrote the original treaty. He wasn't going to be weaker than they had been. He wouldn't be stopped by these stupid dragons. How dare they take his money and imprison him? He was going to get those dragons once and for all.

As Oscar and the others arrived at the palace and Fergus and his men were taken into custody, Oscar let the rest of the dragons know what Fergus had been thinking. "He's got something else in mind. He'll have to be watched."

"We'll let Sapphire and King Bertram know about this," said Foster.

Once the dragons were all gone and things were quiet again, Sapphire turned to Raymond and said, "Well, you can see what we have. Most of the caves around the outside of the grazing fields are still intact. But we have no land that can be farmed or used for livestock. Do you have any suggestions?"

Raymond walked around the Aerie before he spoke. Finally, he said, "My father has shown me the extent of your newly drawn boundaries, so I believe you have more options than you had before. I would like some time to draw up plans for you, but I think you could have several flat areas, maybe one for cattle, one for goats, and one for sheep. The land isn't exactly the best for crops, but there are some spots that, if a few trees were cleared, would work. And with judicious clearing of trees, you would have lumber that would fetch a good price in various villages."

"Wonderful," said Sapphire. "Feel free to draw up whatever vision you have. And I think widening the trail between here and Dragonwind would be helpful and help bring us all closer together."

"Definitely," said Raymond. He began making notes and drawings as he walked around the Aerie.

Harmony, a sea-green dragon who was in charge of the youngest dragons, hurried up to Illyra and Fryzal. "Fryzal, are you OK?"

Fryzal, nestled in Illyra's arms, looked over at Harmony and said, "I found my person. This is Illyra."

Harmony rubbed the top of Fryzal's head and said, "I can see that."

Illyra said, "I'm sorry Fryzal worried you, but Blossom, Ty, and Lyra have all checked her out and said that she will make a full recovery."

Harmony smiled and said, "I'm so glad. She's given us a run for our money in her six months. I'm sure she'll make life interesting, whatever happens."

Sapphire joined the group as she said, "Fryzal only hatched six months ago, but she's always done things her way."

Harmony concurred. "We were worried about her at first because she's so small. I mean, you wouldn't be able to pick up any of the other dragons her age. They're all much bigger. But Fryzal has matured intellectually and emotionally much faster than they have."

"Interesting," said Illyra. "I wonder why."

"I keep telling them that I will grow when I'm ready," said Fryzal. "And face it, if I were bigger, I would have been killed in that explosion. I barely fit in that tiny space between the rocks."

Everyone chuckled at that, but Harmony said, "If you had stayed where you belong, you wouldn't have been in any danger from the explosion."

"But I was where I belonged," protested Fryzal. "How else was I going to find Illyra and Chauncey?"

There was much shaking of heads at this comment, but Illyra just said, "I would have found you no matter where you were. You didn't need to put yourself in danger."

"Maybe," said Fryzal with doubt in her voice.

Ty put a hand on Fryzal to send healing magic into the tiny dragon, and then he exclaimed, "You are really healing quickly. I think your leg will support you now. The break appears to be healed."

Illyra gently placed Fryzal on the ground so she could test Ty's pronouncement. As they all watched, Fryzal, who was about half the size of Chauncey, took some tentative steps and then let out a big whoop of joy. "It is healed. Thank you, Ty."

Ty said, "I don't think I can take all the credit, but I'm glad. Now let me check the wing."

Fryzal held still obediently so Ty could examine her. Ty said, "The wing is also much better. I would like to leave the brace on for a bit longer, though."

"That's OK," said Fryzal. "I'm still a bit young to fly, so I don't mind."

Oscar, Foster, and the other dragons who had taken the prisoners back to the palace returned to report to King Bertram. Oscar said, "The prisoners are all in the castle dungeon, sire." Oscar then told them what he'd learned from Fergus.

"Thanks, Oscar, and the news that Fergus is still plotting is troubling but not unexpected," said the king. "However, for now I think we should be deciding where we are going for the night."

Raymond came over at that point and said, "Father, I would like to stay here to work on my plans, if that's OK."

Sapphire said, "You are most welcome to stay here if you'd like."

Raymond said, "Oh, that would be great if I'm not needed at the palace."

King Bertram said, "I think your number-one priority needs to be the Aerie repairs. I need to get back to the palace and sort out Fergus and his men, but you are welcome to stay here for as long as needed."

And so it was decided that Raymond would stay at the Aerie, Bertram would return to the palace with Oscar's help, and everyone else would head back to Dragonwind.

CHAPTER 12

REPAIRS

The next week produced amazing results. Raymond had plenty of ideas but discovered that those ideas were put into effect with very little help from him. The path from the Aerie to Dragonwind seemed to widen without help. Six tall trees did have to be removed, but the slope of the path became more gentle, much wider, and smoother and cleaner without any assistance. Some of the trees appeared to move on their own, and Raymond could feel the path take on a life of its own.

"You know," said Raymond to Illyra, Chauncey, and Fryzal one afternoon, "if I didn't think this sounded absurd, I'd say that the path has decided to open up all on its own. I suspect the only reason we needed to remove six trees was to give the dragons good-quality lumber to bargain with for livestock."

Fryzal chuckled before saying, "I'm thinking that's exactly what happened."

Illyra said, "Remember Althea said it was important for the dragons to receive help from the merchants and villagers. I suspect that's exactly what we're seeing."

"I can't wait to see what the land will do next," said Raymond. "It does seem to like my ideas, but it also seems able to execute those ideas nearly by itself. So many changes during the night."

Just then they saw more wagons coming up the path from Dragonwind. The wagons were filled with dirt designed to fill out the bomb crater. Once the dirt was dumped, the wagons would be loaded with rocks to be taken to various villages, as all of a sudden everyone seemed to want to have rock walls or even build entire cottages out of quarried rocks.

Jeb and Kyle were each driving a wagon, and when they'd put them in position to be unloaded and then reloaded, they came over to talk with Raymond, Illyra, Chauncey, and Fryzal. As they looked at the group, Jeb said, "Fryzal, you've grown a lot since I saw you, and that was just two days ago."

Fryzal seemed to glow, and her many rainbow colors nearly blinded them all. "Thanks, Jeb. I kept telling Harmony and the others that I would grow when the time was right. I couldn't do it before the explosion. But now, I no longer need to stay small. I'll be the right size shortly."

"That's amazing," said Raymond.

"Not really," said Fryzal. "It's just the way it is meant to be."

"Maybe," said Illyra, "but that doesn't make it any less amazing. And Ty says Fryzal's completely healed from the explosion, both her wing and her leg."

Fryzal hopped up and down and twirled to prove the truth of Illyra's words. Chauncey tried to dance with the dragon, who now was the same size as Chauncey. Everyone laughed at the comical scene.

Then Jeb said, "Well, I suspect the wagons have been emptied and re-loaded, so we better head out."

The group headed back to the center of the Aerie just as Ty and Criseda landed near the crater, which was now barely a dip in the ground. Greetings were exchanged, and then Jeb and Kyle got their wagons moving back down the path.

Ty and Criseda looked around at the progress and said, "Wow, so much has happened so fast."

Sapphire looked at Raymond and said, "Raymond has done absolute wonders here."

Raymond said, "I'm glad you like my plans, but we all know that there's a lot more going on than anything I might have suggested."

Ty looked at Fryzal as he said, "Sort of like my healing magic. I did work on Fryzal, but I could never have healed you as quickly as you've done. And I certainly couldn't have made you grow as fast as you have."

Fryzal seemed to blush, all her rainbow colors nearly dancing, and said, "Well, I just knew what to do and that I would heal and grow when the time was right."

Raymond said, "Driselda, have you seen anything like this in any of your historical records?"

"Not just like this," said Driselda, "but the ancient records do mention what the Aerie was like when the dragons were first exiled here, and how quickly it changed, which it had to do if the dragons were to survive."

Illyra added, "And Althea says that magic developed during that time period."

Raymond said, "I would like to study that time if you'll help me, Driselda. And I suspect that you, Illyra, might be able to get more information from Althea. I get the idea that there have been some major turning points in the development of magic as well as with the dragon-human interactions."

"Certainly," said Driselda.

"I agree," said Illyra.

"But aren't you too busy with this repair project?" asked Ty.

"Honestly," said Raymond, "not really. Once I'd drawn out my ideas and Sapphire tweaked them, the land seems to have taken over the execution of them. Wouldn't you agree, Sapphire?"

Sapphire nodded and said, "Yes, I would. I think that the land itself leaves just enough for humans to accomplish to strengthen the bonds between our species. Althea told us that. And it makes us feel as if we are somehow involved in the changes. That's probably good for us all, but look at how the path changed, basically overnight, to the point where trees moved out of the way, and the path became practically a thoroughfare between here and Dragonwind and even beyond. One day it will be an easy stroll to the capital."

"It is quite amazing," said Ty. "Criseda and I were noticing that as we flew in from the capital."

"I really like engineering and planning things, like making Bergamen's wing extension," said Raymond, "or figuring out how to divert a river, and I probably always will. But now I'm totally fascinated with the history of Estrea and how it's changed and been changed by magic. I know that my father has some telepathic abilities, at least over short distances, so I know that means we are descended from dragon riders, and I would really like to know how."

Driselda said, "I can help you with that. I've got records going back to that time."

Illyra said, "If you give me names, I could ask Althea about them as well."

Raymond looked excited and said, "I'd really like that. I'm going to stay here and write up how the Aerie is changing, as an observer. I think Aloysius would be interested in my account."

Driselda smiled and said, "I would be also. I will enjoy working with you. I, too, am finding this fascinating."

Ty listened to this interchange and smiled. He loved it when people got excited over history. But then he remembered he had information for them from King Bertram. "I look forward to hearing what you discover," he said, "but I also want to let you all know what the king has decided about Fergus and his buddies."

They nodded, and he went on. "Bertram was waiting to decide on their punishment until we could see how Fryzal healed and also how the repairs went. Well, it is obvious that Fryzal is healed and thriving."

Fryzal did another fancy twirl, and everyone laughed. Then Ty continued. "From what I can see and what Raymond and Sapphire have told me, the repairs are incredible, more like a total do-over of the Aerie. And your boundaries have grown exponentially. In fact, the king gets requests several times a week for more cities and towns to join.

"It seems, therefore, that while what Fergus did or tried to do is totally reprehensible, the Aerie is actually in a better, stronger position, and so are the many villages and towns that have joined with you. So the king felt that with Fergus's payment, both the money he got from Malcolm and what the selling of his horses and supplies brought in, Fergus has done enough. He's now freed Fergus and his men, telling them to get out of the capital."

"That sounds fair," said Sapphire. "You are right: we are in a much better position now than we were before Fergus discovered the ancient treaty. I wouldn't have thought it possible, and I hope you, Driselda, and Raymond will be able to find out how this has happened, but as long as Fergus causes no more trouble, I'm satisfied that his punishment was sufficient. After all, he's shown time and again that all he cares about is money, and he's paid a hefty price already."

Driselda reminded the group that Fergus was just the latest in a long list of those who'd tried to control others for their own gain, all the way back to when Esme was forced to work for The Wraith, followed by Jasper's father's bid for power, and then money lenders like Claude and his brother taking over the tunnels and usurious money lending. Unfortunately, Estrea has suffered time and again from those who saw power and money as the only worthwhile goals.

The others nodded at this reminder of the past history of Estrea and how Fergus was just attempting to continue the pattern.

Sage and Star, who were on the edge of this conversation, added, "And Star has been flying over our old home as well as Fergus's business south of the capital. Star, what have you seen?"

Star said, *Rains, winds, and floods. Also earthquakes.*

Sage said, "The bottom line is that the land is not happy with Fergus and his pals. His workers are seeking refuge in the capital. He's not going to be able to keep his business going unless he changes the way he operates, and knowing him, I don't think that is likely."

"Well, he only has himself to blame," said Illyra.

"True," said Sage, "but he's not going to see it that way. He's going to see himself as the victim, and he will feel cornered and trapped. That will make him even more dangerous."

"I don't see what he can do," said Illyra.

Sapphire said, "If I were to guess, and obviously it is a guess since I don't actually know him, you two are his likeliest targets. After all, this all started when the two of you left his house and stood up against him."

"I'm staying here at the Aerie with Fryzal and Chauncey," said Illyra. "He can't get to me here."

"I'm going back to the palace to help the queen reach out to other wives who might be suffering abuse as I was," said Sage. "Miranda and I will work with her, but I'm sure we'll be safe in the palace."

"Well, just be aware," said Sapphire. "I agree with Bertram that Fergus has paid his current debt. But I have to admit I'm not convinced that he will see it that way. He seems to me to be an angry, vindictive man, and that makes him very dangerous."

"Remember what Oscar said about Fergus's thoughts," said Sapphire. "He's definitely planning something else. He'll need to be watched carefully."

"And don't forget what I saw, or thought I saw, at the council meeting, where Zythrym seemed to be egging him on," said Illyra. "I have a feeling that Zythrym is the real power behind all this, although I'm not sure why. But he sure hates not only dragons, but also my mom and me."

"We won't forget," said Sapphire.

CHAPTER 13

NEW INFORMATION

Ty and Criseda flew back to the capital that evening to report to King Bertram, and Sage and Star flew with them. Miranda, Molly, and Malcolm had traveled there a few days earlier, and Sage was looking forward to catching up with them. She was eager to reach out to others who were potentially in the position she had been. She felt so much more confident now, after leaving Fergus. Of course, being healed also helped her, but mostly, she felt the power that comes from owning her own life, making her own choices, and finding ways to help others. She was determined that she would make a difference to others, beginning with abuse victims, especially the wives of rich men.

And she was thrilled that Illyra now had two bonded partners, Chauncey and Fryzal. She applauded their decision to stay up in the Aerie, because she knew what her former husband was capable of doing.

The group entered the palace to find both Bertram and Elicia waiting for them. Sage and Star went off with Elicia, and Ty and Criseda followed Bertram into his office. They all made themselves comfortable, and then Ty reported.

"The repairs are going at an astounding rate," began Ty. "There's something magical going on, and no one is quite sure what it is. Raymond has become fascinated with the history of the Aerie and plans to stay up there and work with Driselda."

Bertram nodded and said, "I'm not surprised. And I think that will be good training for him as my heir."

Just then, there was a knock on the office door. Bertram called, "Enter," and was surprised to see Aloysius come in.

"Aloysius," said Bertram. "What has brought you out of your tower?"

Aloysius walked in and sat in a chair next to Ty before he said, "I have a favor to ask." He held up a manuscript and said, "I've been rereading Tobias's writings. You may recall that he is the most competent and accurate of the ancient historians."

Both Bertram and Ty nodded. Aloysius continued. "I've been hearing about the strange doings up at the Aerie, and I think that Tobias found something similar when the dragons were banished in the first place. I'd like to take my findings to the Aerie to confer with Driselda. Would that be possible?"

"Certainly," said Bertram. "Do you have anything you would like to share with us now?"

"Well," said Aloysius a bit hesitantly, "I wouldn't want to speak without more information, but I think…I mean, you know how we've always rather glossed over the arrival of the Ribendi? Just saying that they were the precursors of dragons, that the dragons evolved from them?"

"Yes," said Ty. "I always thought that was a bit unsatisfactory. Sage has mentioned it too, that there is a gap in our knowledge about the relationship between the Ribendi, the land, and the dragons."

"Well, I think Tobias was bothered by it as well," said Aloysius, "And I think some of his thoughts might give us some idea about what really was going on. I'm also hoping that Illyra's dream connections with her long-ago grandmother might allow us to ask Althea some questions."

"Wow," said Ty. "That sounds exciting. Criseda and I were planning to fly back today. Would that work for you?"

"That would be perfect," said Aloysius. "I want to show this to Driselda," he said, pointing at the manuscript, "and I also want to ask Illyra to ask Althea some questions. If I can catch her before she goes to sleep tonight, maybe she'd be willing to try contact. I do think this is important. We will get a better idea of what's currently going on at the Aerie."

"Works for me," said Ty. "Say in about fifteen minutes?"

"I'll wait in the entryway.," said Aloysius. "I was hoping for this and so packed a small overnight bag and brought it all the way down from my tower so I wouldn't have to do the stairs again right away."

With that, Aloysius stood and left the office to wait for Ty and Criseda.

Ty then turned to Bertram and said, "Well, that does sound interesting. I've never been happy with the way the Ribendi have been glossed over in our accounts of dragon evolution, or even the arrival of the Ribendi on our planet. Maybe with the access we now have to Althea, we'll be able to discover something more."

Bertram smiled and said, "And I already heard from Raymond that he's hoping to get more information about our ancestry with the dragon riders. My telepathic abilities are pretty minor, as you know, but it does mean that we have a link there. I think Raymond wants to know more. We also know that magical gifts sometimes take a while to develop. I think, secretly, Raymond is hoping he might develop at least as much as I have. Bertram was quiet for a few minutes before he said, "I hope he isn't too disappointed if that's not the case."

"Raymond has a good head on his shoulders," said Ty. "I'm sure whatever we find out, he will take it in stride even if it proves to be disappointing."

Bertram nodded and said, "I know. Meanwhile, is there anything else that you want to report?"

Ty stood and walked over to the map of Estrea on the wall of the office. "As you know, the Aerie is now covering a considerable area of Estrea, from the entire far north and then reaching through the middle of Estrea to the center, where we are now."

"Yes," said Bertram as he stood to stand with Ty. "In addition, I've received requests from the towns and villages to the east of the central corridor. So far, I've honored all requests, as I think ultimately, we're going to be forming a new country that is a combination of the Aerie and Estrea. I've even thought about calling it 'Aerestrea.'"

"Cool," said Ty. "I know that's down the road, and that governments would have to change, but I see where you're coming from. Well, I've gotten a report from Star, and I'm sure she'll fill you in, now that she and Sage are here, but the southwestern corner of Estrea is suffering really strange weather. It started with the landslide on Malcolm's lands, but it is spreading."

"Yes," said Bertram, "I've heard the same thing, and we have an unusual influx of refugees from that area seeking sanctuary here."

"And that area is controlled by Fergus and his fellow barons. I would suggest having Star keep an eye on it," said Ty. "I'm sure none of us trust Fergus to behave. That was one reason why I was glad that Illyra, Chauncey, and Fryzal decided to stay in the Aerie. They will be easier to protect there."

"Yes," said Bertram, "and we'll look after Sage and Star."

"It might be good to activate the fox telepathic network so that we can contact you quickly when Oscar and Foster are in Dragonwind," said Ty.

Bertram chuckled before saying, "Oscar and Foster are on top of that already. They've picked a lovely fox named Olivia who lives in the forest behind the palace. The two of us practice sending messages each day, and we've gotten quite good. I can reach her telepathically even from inside the palace, and I can hear her, as long as she's on the edge of the forest."

"Excellent," said Ty. "Then Criseda and I will head to Dragonwind, taking Aloysius with us, and I'll keep you posted on what we learn."

▲

Ty and Criseda flew directly to the Aerie with Aloysius, landing outside Driselda's cave. She came out to meet them and was thrilled to see Aloysius. Ty jumped down off Criseda and then helped the elderly historian down. Ty was pleased to see Raymond, Illyra, Fryzal, and Chauncey coming out of Driselda's cave as well.

Driselda and Aloysius looked at each other, and they both started talking at the same moment, obviously excited to share news. After a moment, Driselda said, "You go first, Aloysius."

"I've brought Tobias's history," began Aloysius, "and I think he has something to say about the Ribendi that might be relevant to what's happening here."

"Excellent," said Driselda. "And we've been thinking of a list of questions we want Illyra to ask Althea."

"That was my thought as well," said Aloysius. "I think we need to know a lot more about the Ribendi. Who were they? How did they get here? What is their relationship with the dragons? Oh, there's so much."

Raymond spoke up, loudly, so he could get a word in between the two very excited historians, "And how does that relate to the magic that is obviously repairing the Aerie? I mean, yes, I did have a plan, but I'm not the one executing it."

"Precisely," said Aloysius, who then smiled at the look of surprise on Raymond's face. "I think Tobias here," he said, pointing to the manuscript, "suspected something all those centuries ago."

"Shall we go into my cave and get more comfortable?" suggested Driselda.

"Thank you, my dear," answered Aloysius.

Ty looked at the group and said, "Well, you obviously don't need me. I'll go check in with Sapphire."

Criseda watched the group head into Driselda's cave and said, "I don't think they even heard you. They're off in their own little world. Let's hope they can get some answers. Or at the very least, that they can come up with questions that Althea is willing to answer."

Ty laughed and said, "For sure."

The two of them turned toward the center of the Aerie to look for Sapphire. They found her with a group of merchants and several wagons. She was saying, "We really appreciate all you are doing for us."

"We're happy to do it," said one of the merchants. "Turns out that Fergus and his friends thought that they could keep controlling us, but we quickly disabused him of that notion. Malcolm is keeping the books for your repairs, and that's where the money you got from Fergus went. Malcolm sees that everyone is paid promptly and fairly. We've never been treated like that before, so we are very happy to be supplying you."

"But that should be how things are always done," said Sapphire in a puzzled tone.

"You would think so," said the merchant. "But the reality is very different. Crooks like Fergus tack on all sorts of extra charges, and then they don't pay us in cash or even comparable goods, such as the lumber you traded for livestock. Instead, they just give us a credit, for less than the bill, and that credit is only good for their stores, which charge outrageously high prices. That's how they keep control over all their workers, who are in debt to the company forever."

"But that's nothing more than slavery," said Sapphire.

"It is," said the merchant. "But it's fast coming to an end, because King Bertram is paying off their debts, and they are then fleeing to the capital, which, as you know, is now part of the Aerie. Soon," concluded the merchant with a chuckle, "Fergus and the others won't have any workers. Serves them right."

"Well, rest assured," said Sapphire, "dragons will always pay promptly and fairly."

"You have a very honest bookkeeper in Malcolm," said the merchant. "He's so happy to have his family safe and to be working for you and Bertram. He's doing a fabulous job, and he's well aware, from personal experience, just how Fergus and the others operated. Makes it easy for him to take workers away from them."

"Good," said Sapphire. "And again, thank you."

The merchant tipped his hat to Sapphire, and once all the wagons were loaded with more stone, the group headed back down the path.

Sapphire then turned to Ty and Criseda and shook her head. "I can't imagine how Fergus has been able to stay in business."

"When they all use the same methods, workers are trapped and have no choice," said Ty. "But that is changing fast now."

"So, what did you find out from Bertram?" Sapphire asked, and Ty and Criseda brought her up to speed, including sharing just how excited Aloysius and Driselda were.

Sapphire chuckled and said, "I've seen those two when they get excited. It is a sight to behold."

▲

Late that afternoon, once Driselda and Aloysius had decided on a reasonable list of questions for Illyra to ask Althea, Illyra, Fryzal, and Chauncey went back to Blossom's cave in Dragonwind. Aloysius and Raymond stayed with Driselda, who'd fixed a spot in her cave for human visitors.

That night, Illyra, Fryzal, and Chauncey slept on the big bed, each of them reaching out to Althea.

It wasn't long before Althea appeared. She said, "So I've been watching you this afternoon. I wondered just how long it would be before you started searching for answers. Aloysius is correct. You do need to know a lot more about the Ribendi if you are going to make any sense out of what's going on now. I never shared much of that with Sage, as the knowledge didn't seem important before now."

Illyra said, "Can you help us?"

Althea said, "If you'd asked me while I was alive, I would have said no. But over the centuries, I've searched for answers, and I think that now, I have a pretty good handle on things. Here's what I think happened, and yes, some of it is still guesswork, but it does make sense.

"The Ribendi were, I believe, non-corporeal. They didn't have bodies as we know them. And they traveled between worlds in something like dreams, as I'm doing here with you."

Illyra said, "Really? Then how did they help, or do anything, or evolve into dragons?"

Althea let out a laugh as she said, "That's one reason it has taken me so long to figure this all out. They traveled to developing worlds, staying only long enough to plant ideas in the existing life forms to nudge them in a progressive direction.

"Then they would drift off to another such world. But something happened when they arrived here, not only on this planet, but specifically in Estrea, the northern area of this planet. I'm not sure what was different here at that time, but I think it was because they found a number of sentient species. They worked not just with humans, much as some humans would like to believe. Dogs, foxes, cats, moose, and others were receptive to contact. And I suspect that's what made things change.

"Here's where I have lots of leaps of faith, but I think the Ribendi were tired of being non-corporeal. I think they hungered for a home. And I think, but I can't be sure, that they decided to take a form that didn't already exist on this world."

Chauncey said, *Dragons.*

"Spot on," said Althea. "I think that's how dragons came to be. And I think that some Ribendi intelligence and memory stayed in the new form, and that's why the dragons have always felt that they were descendants of the Ribendi, although they never knew how.

"I also think that the land itself bonded to the dragons and any who cherished them. After all, it was, I believe, the land itself that attracted the Ribendi. And if I'm right that the Ribendi then decided to stay and evolve into the dragons, then the connection between the dragons and the land would have been very strong. It's reasonable that the land would bond with any who cared about the dragons."

Illyra said, "Like the first dragon riders."

Althea said, "That's what I believe. Because the land took it very badly when the dragons were banished to the Aerie. And just as you are seeing today, the land itself reformed to suit the dragons, giving them and their human companions a spot where they could actually thrive, not just exist."

"Wow," said Fryzal. "But it does fit what's going on now."

Althea smiled at the young dragon as she said, "That it does. It also fits with all the things that the land is doing to those it doesn't like. Hence the landslide at Malcolm's."

"OK," said Illyra, "I think that covers most of our list of questions. If you don't mind, Raymond would like to know if you know who he's descended from. His father, King Bertram, has a weak telepathic ability. I think Raymond is hoping maybe he'll develop that as well. But whether or not that's true, he would just like to know something about his ancestors."

Althea thought for a while before finally saying, "You know that the inheritance branches from the original riders have branched off many times."

Illyra nodded, and Althea continued, "And last year you learned about Fen and his ancestor Obadiah, who was bonded to a dragon named Jade."

Again, Illyra nodded. Finally, Althea said, "Well, Fen isn't the only one who can trace his lineage back to Obadiah. So can King Bertram and hence all his offspring."

"Wow," said Fryzal. "That's cool."

Althea said, "For sure. And while Bertram doesn't have really strong telepathic skills, he has exceptional leadership skills, which require using influence to get others to make the right decisions. I think that Raymond has those same skills. Furthermore, I think Lance does too, and maybe the younger siblings. It is also possible that, put in the right situation, Raymond may demonstrate more magical gifts. That isn't for sure, but it's possible.

"Now, I think I've given you enough for tonight, and enough to keep Driselda, Aloysius, and Raymond satisfied. So get some sleep, my darlings, and we'll talk more another time."

CHAPTER 14

BONDING

The next morning, Illyra, Chauncey, and Fryzal couldn't wait to get up to the Aerie and give the others the news from their dream. When they arrived, they went directly to Driselda's cave. They greeted Driselda, Raymond, and Aloysius, and then Illyra said, "You'll never guess what we learned."

Driselda and Aloysius looked up from an ancient manuscript they had been examining as Raymond moved closer to the table they were working at, and Aloysius said, "Please let us know."

Fryzal said, *"It's amazing. We learned that the Ribendi were non..."*—she stuttered—*"non-something."*

Illyra laughed and looked at Fryzal, who was now taller than she was, and said, "Non-corporeal."

"Yeah, that," said Fryzal.

Driselda and Aloysius looked at each other and then Aloysius said, "Tell us all."

Illyra proceeded to tell the three of them everything they had learned, aided by both Fryzal and Chauncey.

Driselda and Aloysius were quiet for a few minutes, and then Driselda said, "So the Ribendi *designed and created* dragons from their own non-corporeal bodies and powers."

Illyra said, "That's what Althea thought, anyway."

Aloysius said, "That fits with what Tobias thought, or so we now think. He didn't say it so directly, but our old idea that the Ribendi evolved into dragons seems incorrect. He didn't actually believe that that had happened."

Driselda nodded in agreement before saying, "And Althea felt that they designed dragons because they were a new species not found on this planet already."

"Yes," said Illyra. "That was her reasoning."

"But what happened to the Ribendi?" asked Driselda. "Did they then move on to another planet? Do you know?"

No, said Chauncey. *I think Althea indicated that the Ribendi evolved or changed themselves into the dragons. So they would never have left, but their powers fed into both the dragons and the land, enhancing everything.*

Fryzal said, "We will clarify that next time we speak with Althea."

Driselda laughed and said, "I'm sure you will. However, Fryzal, you need to head to school now as you're going to be late."

Fryzal grumbled but left quickly.

Driselda continued, "Meanwhile, this information goes a long way toward explaining what happened during the original exile. Apparently the Ribendi found something special about either this planet or this part of the planet. And we were right, Aloysius, that it is the land itself that is causing a great deal of the changes, and probably also the weather anomalies that are attacking those whom the planet finds troublesome or destructive."

"Yes," said Aloysius. "It would appear that the planet doesn't want to be messed with. And it obviously doesn't like anyone who tries to harm not only the dragons but also anything that interferes with the synergy between the dragons and other species."

"That is interesting," said Illyra. "I wonder what the Ribendi found at other planets they helped. Do you think that there were fewer different species on those? What attracted the Ribendi to do more here than they apparently did on other planets? Was it the very land itself, which it seems is sentient also? I guess we'll have to find out if Althea knows."

Raymond hesitated but finally asked, "Did you find out anything about my ancestors? I mean, I know that probably isn't high on the list of questions. Just wondering."

Illyra smiled at him and said, "Actually we did. And Driselda, you're probably able to help us as well. Althea said that there were only a relatively small number of original dragon riders. She thought there were fewer than fifty. But we know that there are many more who would be descended from them and hence potentially have magic."

Driselda nodded and said, "That is true. Genealogical trees can expand quite quickly depending on the number of offspring each generation has."

"Althea was apparently most interested in those who went on to become major power figures in Estrea, such as your family, Raymond," said Illyra. "Apparently Obadiah, who was bonded to a dragon named Jade, had five sons. So right away there are five branches from his line. We already know that Fen belongs to one of those branches. Fen got zer influencer magic from Obadiah. Well, it turns out you're on another one of those branches. Althea thinks that one reason your father is such a beloved king and such a good ruler is that he has some of that influencer magic, and just as Fen only uses it for good, so does your father."

"Wow," said Raymond.

"Yes, and Althea suspects that both you and Lance have some influencer abilities as well," Illyra concluded.

"But I thought that anyone with magic always had telepathic magic," said Raymond.

Driselda said, "Well, Bertram does, although it's not super strong. But I suspect that's more because he's never used it enough to develop that strength. And look at the way you're able to convince people when you propose your engineering projects. You've done some pretty remarkable things, especially moving the Rocking Rocks river to clean out the old mines, or rebuilding the slum area in the capital. I've always thought your ability to organize so many different groups to accomplish those tasks was incredible, especially for someone your age."

Raymond looked embarrassed and said, "People just wanted to help."

"Maybe," said Driselda, "but I can understand it better now. I think Althea has a point. And you're still young. You may yet develop telepathic abilities."

Raymond smiled at that.

Illyra said, "I'm going to go meet Fryzal, as she's done with school for the day. Would you like to come with Chauncey and me?"

"Sure," said Raymond.

As they walked from Driselda's to the school and nursery where Fryzal was, Raymond said, "So what does Fryzal learn at her school?"

"She's just finishing up her education," said Illyra. "She's way ahead of the other dragons her age. And now, thanks to her growth spurt, she's also bigger than the others. She only has to finish Dragon History, which she loves; Dragon Rules, which she's not fond of; and Dragon Etiquette, which she really dislikes."

Raymond chuckled at that. Fryzal came charging toward them, saying, "Guess what! I passed all three of my classes. I'm done with school."

"Wow," said Illyra. "Congratulations."

Raymond started to say the same thing, but then stopped and appeared to be listening to something. Then he said, "Who are you?"

"Who is who?" asked Illyra.

"Someone was just talking to me, in my head, asking me to come to him," said Raymond with a puzzled expression on his face.

Fryzal said, "I didn't hear anyone."

Illyra said, "I also didn't hear anyone. Are you sure?"

Raymond said, "Not exactly. I thought I heard something, but I could almost feel the voice, if that makes any sense."

Illyra looked at Raymond carefully and said, "That sounds as if it was telepathy. Can you try to find out who is talking to you?"

Raymond said, "I don't know how to do that."

"Just think about what you'd like to ask. I'd start with asking, 'Where are you?'"

Raymond did just that, and a small voice said, *I'm behind the school.*

Raymond moved to the rear of the school, followed by the others. There they saw a bright yellow dragon standing by himself. The dragon said, "I've been waiting for you. My name is Gundryd. Would you want to be my person?"

Raymond looked startled but finally said, "Would you want to be with me?"

Gundryd said, "Definitely. The land spoke to me and told me that you would be good to me."

"The land told you," said Raymond, looking baffled.

"Yes," said Gundryd. "The land really likes what you have been doing over the last few years, from cleaning up the old mines to fixing the slums, and now helping the dragons rebuild the Aerie. And I've just graduated from school. I'm the same age as Fryzal, and I stood up for her when she was still really small but also really bright, so the land said that if I wanted, I could bond with a human. I do want, and the land said that you would be the best choice because you are so in tune with the land. So will you?"

Raymond hurried over to Gundryd and looked him right in the eyes, saying, "I would be honored. Thank you for asking."

Gundryd smiled and said, "The land also told me that you are new to magic and telepathy but that I could help you learn. I tried it out when you were around at the front of the building, and you did hear me, didn't you?"

Raymond smiled and said, "Yes, I did."

Sapphire came over to the group, saying, "I understand that Gundryd has chosen you, Raymond. That is wonderful."

Raymond looked surprised but said, "Yes, he has. I can't believe it."

"Well, I can," said Sapphire, "and I think Gundryd has made an excellent choice."

"I didn't even know that I had any magic," said Raymond.

"Well, your father does," said Sapphire. "And now we know that he probably has more than he knew, being descended from Obadiah. So it makes sense that since he has five children, at least one of them, maybe more, would also have magical abilities."

"I guess," said Raymond. "I never thought of it like that. I'm just kinda blown away by all this."

"I can imagine," said Sapphire. "May I suggest that you stay with Gundryd in his cave for now, and the two of you can get to know each other?"

Illyra and Fryzal cheered for the new pair as Gundryd raced off to his cave, followed by a slightly bewildered Raymond. Then Illyra looked at Sapphire and said, "What do you think Bertram will make of this?"

Sapphire smiled and said, "I think he'll be very happy for Raymond. And honestly, I'm not surprised by this development. After all, it appears that the Aerie and Estrea are combining themselves. Ty told me that Bertram has already come up with a name, Aerestrea. And Raymond is his heir, so having an heir bonded to a dragon would cement the bond between the two nations."

"That's true," said Illyra. "But my father will be furious when he finds out."

Fryzal said, "You've got that right."

"I wouldn't be surprised if the southwestern part of Estrea broke away, at least for a bit, and formed its own independent land with Fergus as the leader," said Sapphire.

"I think it would be too small an area to survive as its own country," said Illyra.

"I'm sure you are right," said Sapphire. "But that won't stop him from trying."

Just then Fen, Edward, and Bergamen arrived in the central clearing in the Aerie and raced over to Sapphire. Fen said, "Did I hear it right? Do I have a distant cousin? Did he just bond with a young dragon?"

Sapphire laughed and said, "Yes, to all your questions. King Bertram and hence all of his offspring are also related to Obadiah as you are. And Gundryd and Raymond are now bonded. Gundryd asked Raymond, and Raymond accepted. Gundryd is now helping Raymond with his telepathic skills."

"Oh, that's wonderful," said Fen, as Blossom with Martha on her back landed next to them.

"Did we hear correctly?" asked Martha.

Sapphire laughed and said, "Yes, you did."

Martha said, "We need to have a party. Everyone will want to welcome the pair. May we have it here, Sapphire? Now that the new path is so much better, people will be able to get here easily, and it seems appropriate to celebrate here."

Blossom looked at Sapphire and said, "Did you realize what you'd be getting in for when you agreed to annex so much territory?"

Sapphire shook her head and said, "Not entirely, obviously." Then she saw a frown come over Martha's face and quickly added, "But this is a wonderful change. We can celebrate both the repairs and renovations of the Aerie and Raymond and Gundryd's bonding. Would tomorrow work for everyone, do you think?"

Martha looked very relieved and said, "Definitely. Naomi is already baking. Tomorrow lunchtime would be grand."

Sapphire chuckled and said, "Yes, that sounds perfect."

Wilhelmina came into the clearing with Paul on her back, along with Felix, Matthew, and Robert, the three orphans that Paul's mother, Naomi, had agreed to foster. As Wilhelmina stopped in front of Sapphire, the four boys slid off her back and shouted, "Can we see Raymond and Gundryd?"

I'm so sorry, said Wilhelmina. *They're just way too excited. And I know that Raymond is new to telepathy, so I thought maybe I could be of assistance as he learns.*

Sapphire said, "Since you are our planet's strongest telepath, I'm sure you can. And as Blossom has just reminded me, the new renovations to the Aerie as well as the political changes have made the Aerie much more accessible."

That's certainly true, and personally, said Wilhelmina, *I'm much happier with the new, wider path.*

Sapphire laughed before she called to Illyra, "Could you, Chauncey, and Fryzal take these overexcited boys and Wilhelmina to Raymond and Gundryd's cave?"

"I would be happy to," said Illyra. "Follow me!"

Once they had left the center of the Aerie, Sapphire looked at Blossom and Martha as she said, "You were right. We have a lot of changes coming."

Blossom bent one of her front legs so Martha could climb back on her, and once Martha was comfortable, Blossom said, "I'm betting the novelty will wear off, but the news about Raymond is pretty fantastic. I think Criseda, Oscar, and Foster plan to bring Bertram, Elicia, and their four other children here either later today or first thing tomorrow so they can meet Gundryd and congratulate Raymond."

"I suspect tomorrow's party will be lots of fun," said Sapphire.

With that, Blossom and Martha headed back to Dragonwind to make preparations for the festivities.

Gundryd and Raymond were just settling into their cave when the visitors descended on them. Raymond knew everyone, but Gundryd didn't. And Raymond wasn't used to the cave, the bonding with Gundryd, or telepathy, so it was all a bit overwhelming. He looked around the small cave, noticing that it was just one room, but Gundryd had added a few personal touches, including some brightly colored pillows. There were also a couple of ledges, one of which was bigger than he was. As he was trying to absorb all that had just happened, he heard the arrival of more guests.

Wilhelmina took one look at Raymond, realizing immediately that he was in a state of shock, and took charge right away. Paul had been bonded to Wilhelmina for nearly four years, and he was telepathic, so Wilhelmina worked through him to command the other three, who had no magical abilities. It worked reasonably well, as the boys loved her, and Paul spoke with a sterner voice when passing on a command from Wilhelmina. The foster boys knew the difference between what Paul would say and what was a command from Wilhelmina, and they didn't hold it against Paul when he had to tell them what Wilhelmina wanted them to do.

Wilhelmina moved in front of Gundryd and Raymond, standing between them and the rest of the group. *Paul, will you tell them they need to put on their company manners?*

Paul nodded and said, "Stop. You need to calm down. Be respectful and give Raymond and Gundryd some space."

Immediately the other three boys grew quiet. Then Matthew, the eldest, said, "Sorry, Raymond, Gundryd. It's just so exciting."

The others nodded and Raymond said, "I agree. But one at a time would be helpful. Gundryd has never met you. How about you each grab a pillow and sit?"

The boys looked around and noticed all of the big colorful pillows, which looked wonderful to sit on. They each found one they liked, and Illyra, Chauncey, and Fryzal followed suit. Wilhelmina made herself comfortable and then said, *So, Raymond, how're you doing with telepathy? Can I help you?*

Raymond looked startled and then said, *I'm not sure. Can you hear me?*

Paul laughed as he said, *We all can, except for Matthew, Robert, and Felix.*

"Oh, I didn't know," said Raymond.

"It's totally OK," said Illyra. "You can speak telepathically to everyone who has that magic or to just one or a small group, or whatever you want. I'm betting that Wilhelmina can teach you quickly how to do that, how to shield your thoughts, and so forth. You didn't even know you had that gift until Gundryd called to you."

"I sure didn't," said Raymond.

"Why don't Chauncey, Fryzal, and I take Gundryd, Matthew, Robert, and Felix outside so they can get to know Gundryd. That way, Wilhelmina and Paul can help you. Would that be OK? Paul, would you be willing to help Raymond?"

"Yes," said Paul, "Although I would like to get to know Gundryd as well."

Illyra ruffled Paul's hair and said, "I promise. You will. I don't think it will take long for you and Wilhelmina to bring Raymond up to speed, and after all, it's really important, as you know better than most of us, to be able to use telepathy. Remember, if you hadn't also figured it out really fast when you were not quite six, you and your friends would have died in that mine collapse."

"True," said Paul. "We'll make sure he knows what he needs to know, won't we Wilhelmina?"

Definitely, said Wilhelmina. *And thank you, Illyra.*

"My pleasure," said Illyra as she herded the others out of the cave.

Once they were outside, the boys asked Gundryd a ton of questions. Illyra suggested that they take turns, each asking one question, until they were all answered. They agreed, and Robert, as the youngest, began first. "So how old are you?"

"I'm the same age as Fryzal here. We're both just over a year old."

"Can you fly?" asked Felix.

"Yes, we can," said Fryzal, "but we can only carry our bonded partner. We'll get bigger and stronger like Criseda, Sapphire, and the others and eventually be able to carry several passengers."

"How did you know you wanted to bond with Raymond?" asked Matthew.

Gundryd was thoughtful for a few minutes before he said, "That's a hard question to answer. We learned about bonded pairs in school."

Robert interrupted, "You have to go to school?"

Gundryd laughed and said, "Fryzal and I have just passed the last of our exams and graduated, but yes, we did. Anyway, in school we learned about bonded pairs in our history lessons."

Seeing the puzzled looks on the boys' faces, Gundryd described how in ancient times, dragons bonded with humans. Then, after dragons were exiled to the Aerie, only a few humans accompanied them here, and eventually, the practice of bonding died out. Two centuries later, Ty made friends with the dragons, especially Criseda. Gundryd continued to explain that it was Bergamen's mother, Windsong, who could see into the future, who realized that the time had come for dragons to return to the world and again to bond with human riders. So Bergamen and Jasper were the first truly bonded pair in the modern age. Soon after, Sapphire agreed that this was a good idea, and she allowed Ty and Criseda to bond.

Gundryd concluded by saying, "And now we also have Illyra and Fryzal, and me and Raymond."

"But how did you pick Raymond?" asked Matthew.

"Well, the land spoke to me," said Gundryd.

"What?" exclaimed Matthew. "The land doesn't talk."

Gundryd said, "Well it did to me, and I couldn't be happier. Raymond and I are made for each other."

"What about you, Fryzal?" asked Felix.

"I just knew," said Fryzal. "And as Gundryd can tell you, when I was born, I didn't grow as fast as the other dragons."

"Your body didn't," said Gundryd, "but your intelligence sure did. Grew much faster than anyone else's."

"Be that as it may," said Fryzal. "It was as if I knew I'd need to stay small to stay safe, and when Fergus blew up the Aerie, that's just what happened. I wouldn't have survived if I hadn't been able to fit in a very tiny space."

"Unless you'd just stayed in the nursery the way you were supposed to," said Gundryd. "None of us were hurt."

"But then I might not have found Illyra," argued Fryzal.

"I think I would always have found you," said Illyra. "But you certainly made it easier for me."

"And once you found her, you grew so fast," said Gundryd. "I still can't believe how much you've grown in the last month or so. You're just as big as me."

"I think I was helped by the land as well," said Fryzal. "Look how it's changed the Aerie. There's a special magic here."

"You're right about that," said Raymond as he, Paul, and Wilhelmina came out of the cave.

Can you talk to me telepathically now? asked Gundryd.

Definitely, said Raymond, and he laughed.

Wilhelmina said, *He's a really quick learner, and his telepathy is very strong. He even managed to contact Olivia, the fox who lives in the forest outside the palace, to let her know about his telepathy and his bonding so she can tell his parents.*

Paul repeated what Wilhelmina said and added, "But I think they already know, because Olivia said that they were already planning to come here tomorrow for the celebrations. But it was good that Raymond could reach them on his own."

Raymond said, "Thanks, guys, for being our first guests! I think you'd probably better head for home now, but we'll see you at the festivities tomorrow."

"Yeah," said Robert. "Naomi and Martha are cooking like mad, and there's going to be a lot of cake."

"Sounds good," said Raymond.

With that, the three boys climbed back onto Wilhelmina and headed back to Dragonwind, with many shouts of thanks.

CHAPTER 15

CELEBRATIONS

That night, as Illyra, Chauncey, and Fryzal slept in their room at Blossom's, Althea came to them. "I need to let you know that the danger isn't over," she said.

What? asked Chauncey.

"I'm afraid that all the problems that Fergus is having," said Althea, "have just made him more determined. The planet has nearly destroyed his business, and his home in the capital is gone as well. The land managed to cause a very localized earthquake, which only destroyed Fergus's mansion.

"Also, Malcolm isn't the only one of his baron friends who has abandoned him. Most of the others on the king's council who previously had supported Fergus have changed their minds once the land started fighting back. They saw what happened to Malcolm's home, and they didn't want the same thing happening to them, so they have decided not to take sides either for or against Fergus's plan.

"Fergus is planning something, but I haven't been able to find out just what that is. But you all need to be careful. And he does know about Raymond and Gundryd. That's made him really mad because he realizes this means that King Bertram's heir is bonded to a dragon. If he can't stop that, then he will never get rid of the dragons.

"He's totally lost his reason over this, so please be careful, and please let Sapphire, Ty, and King Bertram know what I've found out when you see them tomorrow. He's totally irrational, and that makes him extremely dangerous."

Fryzal said, "We'll be sure to let everyone know. He's really nasty, and that's a shame. He had a beautiful wife and daughter before he totally alienated them."

"Yes," said Illyra. "My mom has now divorced him, and I won't have anything to do with him either. Thanks, Althea, for the warning. We'll spread the word, and we'll be very careful."

The next morning, when Blossom, Illyra, Chauncey, and Fryzal headed toward the path that led to the Aerie proper, they discovered that a lot of villagers had the same idea. The mood was very festive, and several villagers were towing wagons filled with various food items. They saw Martha, who waited for them, saying, "Wagons have already taken tables up to the Aerie. This impromptu celebration seems to have taken on a life of its own."

"Wow," said Fryzal.

Blossom looked at the villagers and said, "It's really heartwarming to see how well the joining of Estrea and the Aerie is going. It's also quite a testimony to the love everyone holds for King Bertram and his family."

"I agree," said Martha. "And they should be arriving any time now."

The parade up to the Aerie was moving at a good pace. The new trail was beginning to take on a well-worn look. Kids were running up and down, chasing each other, and their parents looked relieved that their kids had such a safe space to run off their excess energy.

When Illyra and her companions arrived at the open space in the Aerie, they looked around to see that the tables had been set up over on one side of the space and that the tables were already being filled with everything from casseroles to baked goods, from main dishes to desserts. Each table had a different colored cloth covering it, with lots of them being yellow to celebrate Gundryd's bright yellow scales.

The tables had been arranged by type of food, and Illyra noticed that there were actually two tables for the desserts: pies of every kind, lots of brownies and cookies, and a number of cakes, all saying, "Congratulations, Gundryd and Raymond."

Illyra was glad to see that in addition to various salads, there were plenty of macaroni-and-cheese casseroles, as these were her personal favorites.

The dragons seemed to be enjoying the crowds, and Illyra was amused to see a number of dragons acting as jungle gyms for the younger children to climb on and over. Another group was offering to give short rides to any who wished to see what the world looked like from the back of a dragon.

Illyra looked around for Sapphire. She found her standing off to one side of the clearing, looking fondly at the assembled gathering. Just then, Criseda and Ty landed, and Illyra saw that they were carrying Harriet and Hazel. Once they had helped the girls down, Oscar landed with Sage, Star, Elicia, and Eugene. After that, Foster landed with Bertram and Lance.

Soon, all the new guests were clustered around Raymond and Gundryd. It was heartwarming to see how the family embraced the new addition and how proud both Raymond and Gundryd looked.

Lance looked at his big brother and said, "So you have magic and a dragon! Can I get a ride?"

Raymond laughed and hugged Lance as Gundryd said, "I'd be honored to give you a ride anytime, Lance."

Sapphire looked at the group and said, "Well, Bertram, shall we welcome everyone and get this party going?"

Bertram smiled at Sapphire and said, "We'd better, or all the food will be gone before we get any."

Sapphire nodded and said, "You know, this is not what dragons normally eat. We aren't much for cooking or casseroles or baked goods. But I've got to say, after watching a number of my dragons sampling the wares, I tried a few items and discovered that they were quite tasty. So yes, let's officially open the festivities and then make our way to the food."

Sapphire called out loudly, "Welcome one and all. As she did so, the group quieted and gave her and Bertram their attention. Sapphire continued, "As you know, we are all one country, and for many of you, this is your first visit to the Aerie. Please feel free to look around, and if you have any questions, don't hesitate to ask. Bertram and I are both here to make sure that everyone feels welcome and knows that they belong. Today is a celebration of the new Aerie after the senseless destruction. So many of you helped us rebuild, and there aren't words to thank you for opening your hearts so generously to us."

The audience cheered loudly at this. When they quieted, Sapphire continued, "We are also here to celebrate a dragon-human bonding. Raymond, who has done so much for both our communities, has discovered his heritage, come into his magic, and bonded with Gundryd, who sought Raymond out. Come up here, you two."

Raymond and Gundryd moved toward Sapphire, both of them looking a bit embarrassed by all the attention. Sapphire continued, "I think it is especially wonderful that this bonding occurred as our countries are joining. What do you think, Bertram?"

Bertram, who was standing right with Sapphire, said, "I couldn't agree more. Since my heir is now a dragon rider, we can rest assured that everyone, no matter what their species or abilities, will be treated with respect and kindness, both now and in the future. I would like to propose a name for our newly merged country. Let us be known as Aerestrea, if that is agreeable to you, Sapphire, and your dragons."

There were loud cheers from the entire crowd, both dragons and others. Sapphire said,

"I think that's a wonderful idea. Let's celebrate this by digging into the wonderful food that is before us. And let's get to know each other better. Have fun, and welcome, everyone."

Chauncey let out a bark, and Star flew overhead in agreement. There was a dash for the table and all the delicious food, and soon, everyone was enjoying the festive afternoon.

Illyra, Chauncey, and Fryzal hadn't forgotten their promise to Althea, and as the crowd broke into smaller groups, they worked their way toward Sapphire, Bertram, and Sage. Eventually, Illyra was able to say, "We had a visit from Althea last night."

Immediately, they had everyone's attention. Fryzal said, "We need to be watchful."

Illyra patted Fryzal on one of her wings since she could no longer reach Fryzal's head. Then she said, "Fryzal is correct. All three of us"—she put her other hand on Chauncey—"heard her warning that Fergus isn't done yet. He's apparently very angry."

Star said, *I'd agree with that. I've been flying over his properties, and he's lost everything to weather damage, flooding, and earthquakes.*

Illyra nodded and said, "Althea also said that he's losing support with the other barons who had been supporting him."

Bertram nodded as he said, "I've been receiving more overtures from the southwestern part of Estrea asking for help and pledging allegiance to both Estrea and the Aerie. Bertram paused for a moment before he smiled. "Or should I say pledging allegiance to Aerestrea."

The group chuckled as Bertram continued. "Actually, I was going to suggest that we offer storm damage help to those who contacted me. What do you think, Sapphire?"

"I would heartily concur," said Sapphire. "Look at this gathering, and think back to the council meeting where Humphrey and the others asked to join us. What was behind that move? Why didn't they move to side with Fergus?"

Raymond spoke up, "It was because the likes of Fergus had never cared anything about what happened to them. But you and my father demonstrated repeatedly that you both do care."

"Precisely," said Sapphire. "And they knew that we truly do care. We aren't just doing things with some other ulterior motive. The former slum area is still, over a year later, looking vibrant and healthy. Elicia, you and your crew are still helping those in need. This wasn't a flash-in-the-pan sort of effort. And merchants like Humphrey from other parts of the capital are seeing their businesses grow as well. I say let's head to the southwest first thing tomorrow and help these barons out. Maybe that will turn them away from Fergus and toward a better life."

"Agreed," said Bertram. "Now we will be watchful, Illyra, but we will also enjoy this celebration. Look, over there, isn't that Priscilla and Stella with Mittens? Did you ever think that they would look so safe and happy? Just watch Stella, with Mittens being her eyes, climbing over Oscar. It's wonderful."

Ty agreed and said, "And Wilhelmina is getting a real workout, with those who are a bit too small for dragon rides taking rides on her. Paul is being so gentle with the younger ones. I'm sure he'd like a dragon ride the way Matthew, Felix, and Robert are getting, and we'll have to make sure he does get that, but he's being so patient with the toddlers who want to ride Wilhelmina."

"Oh, look," said Sapphire, "Fen, Edward, and Bergamen are working with Paul. It does my heart good to see so much interaction between all our species."

The others nodded. Then Bertram turned to Raymond and Gundryd and asked, "So, what are you two going to do now that you're a pair?"

"I know that before Gundryd and I bonded, I thought about working with Driselda on the history stuff and figuring out where magic came from and what the land is doing. But we talked with her last night, and she helped us to see that studying the land and doing engineering aren't mutually exclusive. She and Aloysius are going to keep searching the written records, and they'll keep us informed. But we'd both like to keep helping with Mother's group, and it sounds as if there are more areas in need of repair. The land has been pretty insistent that either everyone works together or else. Driselda showed us that we could listen and learn from the land and then share what we learn with her and Aloysius. And we've already talked with Oscar and Foster, who say that there is another cave that we could use that's near the palace. Does that sound OK?"

Elicia gave Raymond a hug and then patted Gundryd as she said, "That sounds better than OK."

Bertram smiled and nodded as he said, "I second that."

Gundryd looked over at Sapphire, who was also smiling. She said, "You and Fryzal have graduated, and it's time for you to find your spot in the world. I think that sounds like an excellent plan. How about you, Fryzal? Have you and Illyra decided what you want to do?"

Chauncey let out a bark, and Sapphire added, "And of course you too, Chauncey."

Illyra laughed and said, "We're going to be guided by Althea. At the moment, she's most worried about what Fergus might be planning, so I think, if it's OK with everyone, and if there's room for us, that we should join the repair crew."

Elicia said, "That's definitely OK, and you three may stay in the palace. Your mother and Star are already staying there, and my younger children will be thrilled to add another dragon and a dog to our population."

With this all settled, the group joined in the festivities. It was wonderful to enjoy all the doings, and they saved their worries for another day. It was a gorgeous sunny day, not too hot or cold, and everyone was happy chatting as the children ran around and played with dragons. But finally, everyone agreed that the day needed to wind down before everyone, adults and children alike, fell asleep where they stood.

At the end of the festivities, the villagers returned to Dragonwind, and King Bertram, his family, Sage, Star, Fen and Edward, Ty and Criseda, Raymond and Gundryd, Illyra, Chauncey, and Fryzal, with the help of Oscar and Foster, all returned to the capital.

CHAPTER 16

More Repairs

As Illyra, Chauncey, and Fryzal slept, they received another visit from Althea. Althea showed them the havoc that the land had wreaked on the southwestern lands of Estrea. There was evidence of storm damage and landslides everywhere. In addition, earthquakes had destroyed a number of buildings and homes. Obviously, there was going to be a lot to do to make the land whole again.

Althea then said, "You remember that the land itself has been fighting back against Fergus and the others. Repairs at the Aerie only happened once that threat had been countered."

Illyra said, "So, what about this area? Will the land allow us to make changes?"

Althea said, "There's more going on here than I've shared with you. I didn't want to scare you, but the danger is extreme. I already told you about the danger from Fergus, and that is a very real danger. He's been thwarted; he feels trapped and defeated, and he thinks that you and your mother are the reason for all his defeats. And he is a very real threat, but not the worst. Have you ever wondered why I've chosen to dream walk with you now? I know I have dream walked with your mother over the years, but if you compared notes with her, you'd soon discover that what I did with her was very different from what I'm doing with the three of you.

"All I did with her was try to bolster her courage so that she stayed with Fergus and kept you safe from him. I also had her stress our family's history so that when the time came for me to work with you directly, you would have some background."

Illyra was quiet for a bit before she said, "So you always knew that I'd be the one who would need your information?"

"Yes," said Althea, "and now I need to tell you why. You see, I'm not the only one from the time of the dragons' original banishment."

"What?" said Fryzal. "What do you mean?"

Althea let out a little chuckle and then said, "I'll explain more, Fryzal. Don't worry. But I can only explain enough to keep you alert. I can't change history by telling you the future, or even hinting at it. But if I don't give you a head's up, so to speak, it could be disastrous for the dragons, humans, all life, even, and the new country of Aerestrea will be doomed from the start."

"That sounds really serious," said Illyra.

"It is," continued Althea. "So I can tell you that as the original dragon riders died out, the land (and I believe you now understand that the land is a major player in our history) told me that I would have a descendent who would be called upon to save the dragons during a time of unrest. That's when I was granted the power to dream walk, which I've now been doing for centuries, making sure that my descendants knew the true history of the early banishment and keeping the records that you have now turned over to Driselda and Aloysius safely.

"When you were born, I knew you were something special. As you grew, I could see that you had some very strong magic. So I helped your mother to foster that and protect you until the time was right. I made sure she had a bonded animal with her through the years. And on that horrible night when your father tried to kill her, I made sure that Star was able to foil that. She, of course, did not know of my actions, as that would have given her information that she couldn't have without causing damage to the timeline.

"And I couldn't come to you, as I've said before, until you were away from Fergus and of age. That's what's gotten us to this point. But there is another from my time, who has chosen a different path. He is actually inhabiting the body of one of the current players in Fergus's plan. I told you about him earlier. He is the one who saw magic as a power he could use to dominate everyone else. He's the one who tried to take over the Aerie, who, when that failed in large part because of me, started to kill off both dragons and riders, and who ultimately was banished."

Who? shouted Chauncey. *I'll stop him.*

Althea said, "Loyal Chauncey. You would try, and I know you will do your best to protect both Fryzal and Illyra, but you would be killed needlessly. Fryzal and Illyra will have to defeat this evil on their own."

"But how?" asked Fryzal.

"I can't tell you that now," said Althea. "I can't even let you know who the spirit is inhabiting. I can only let you know that you need to watch out for the real power behind Fergus. Yes, he's dangerous, and he is the one making the biggest chaos at the moment, but he's not the real power in this equation. He thinks he's running the show. He's a narcissist who thinks he's all important. But in reality, he is being manipulated by another without even realizing it."

Althea then went on to tell them more of her history. During her life, this power-hungry rider fell in love with her, but she didn't want anything to do with him. She saw something dark in his soul and knew that his own dragon was worried. But this rider was very handsome and was seen by most as being a strong leader.

When Althea fell in love with another rider, this dark rider grew violent toward her. He vowed that she would never marry anyone else and that he'd make sure her line ended with her. That was why, once that rider's dragon turned on him for his efforts to take over the Aerie, she and the other riders fought him, and she was instrumental in his near capture. Eventually, he was pushed out of the Aerie but not killed.

So Althea married and had offspring and eventually was granted the power to dream walk with her descendants to keep them safe, as one of them would be needed eventually to defeat the spirit of the evil rider who was seeking not only power and the end of the dragons, but also the end of all Althea's descendants.

Illyra thought about all her father's friends but then shook her head, saying, "How will we know who it is? By any chance is one of Fergus's friends connected to this past rider? I noticed at the council meeting that Zythrym has a real hatred for my mom and me, as well as for the dragons. He seemed to blame me for something."

"I can't give you any more information, but your observations are accurate. I'll share more later, but you need to know that there is going to be an attack soon. The attack will be two pronged, against you and your mother, but one of the attacks will just be a distraction to carry out the other. I can't tell you any more than that. But you must be watchful.

"One more thing. Each of you has strong magic that will play a role. You aren't experienced in using it. In fact, you might not even realize that you have it. But now I'm going to reveal your gifts to each of you. Chauncey, you know that you have all the talents of a dog, but yours are extra strong. Your sense of smell as well as your sense of hearing are much stronger than even the best dog. This makes you a fantastic tracker, a skill you will need when the attacks happen. Make sure you are familiar with the scents of everyone around you at all times.

"Fryzal, you have the ability to teleport yourself. This is a gift that hasn't been seen in centuries, and I know you haven't had time to practice it or strengthen it. However, I believe that the land will guide you. And listen to Gundryd. He will be an invaluable friend, especially since the land can speak to him. That's his magical talent.

"Finally, Illyra, you discovered your other ability, the ability of telekinesis, when you rescued Fryzal. You will need this ability in the coming battle, as this ability will enable you to trap the one who is trying to destroy this world.

"Now," said Althea as they all tried to pepper her with questions, "that is all I can say. In truth, I may have said too much. But you are up against a much older and stronger force, and so I need to make sure you have the tools you need. You can do this, but now, you need to sleep."

As Althea said that, all three of them fell into a deep sleep and didn't wake until morning. When they did wake, it was to find Blossom calling them to breakfast.

"Hurry along, you three," she called. "Bertram and Sapphire want to get everyone moving quickly. I've put breakfast out on the table. Eat quickly and come out onto the green. Dragons are already heading out to survey the damage."

Illyra, Fryzal, and Chauncey did move faster at that news. They gulped down their breakfasts and headed outside. It didn't take long for Sapphire to pair up those needing rides with the dragons who would take them. Illyra would, of course, ride on Fryzal, but she wasn't strong enough yet to take another passenger, so Chauncey was going on Blossom, along with Martha. Others were following Sapphire's instructions, and soon everyone was on their way to the southwestern lands.

As they flew southwest for nearly an hour to the damaged area, Illyra thought about all that Althea had told them last night. As she thought over the recent history of Estrea, now Aerestrea, she could see a pattern to the events. First the dragons isolated themselves after being banished to the Aerie. Then there were a series of crises that necessitated new magics and more interactions between dragons and humans. Finally, the dragons realized—probably thanks to both Windsong and the land's interactions, even though they hadn't realized it at the time—that the problems could only be solved with cooperation.

So far, each of the crises had been met, but there hadn't been a permanent fix. Events seemed to move from crisis to crisis, but each time the bonds between species, especially dragons and humans, grew stronger, as did the magic in the land. Would this crisis finally fix things for good? Could she, Fryzal, and Chauncey really heal things? Illyra just wasn't sure.

▲

When they all arrived, they looked around at the devastation in dismay. "How are we supposed to fix this?" asked Ty.

Just then a group of men came over to them, and Fergus said, "Here to gloat?"

"No," said Bertram. "We're here to offer our help, if you want it, Fergus."

Fergus looked startled and said, "I don't believe it. Why would you try to help us? We're trying to stop all your changes."

"We're hoping that you've seen the error of your ways," said Bertram, "or that you will when we offer help for you without any strings attached."

"No one does that," said Fergus.

"Not true," said the king. "You may not, but not everyone is as selfish as you. Haven't your workers suffered enough? We're here to offer whatever assistance we can. You may take it or not as you wish."

Zythrym came up to Fergus and said, "Come on, Fergus. We could certainly use the brawn of the dragons to clean this mess up. And I understand that Raymond has had great success redesigning damaged lands. We'd be foolish not to take them up on their offer of help. We aren't joining their cause, as some of your other fickle friends have done, but we could use the labor."

Esme had been observing Zythrym carefully, and she spoke telepathically to Ty. *He's lying. He intends to keep us here so he can trap Sage and Illyra. I don't know why, at least not yet, but he wants their power.*

Ty gave no sign that he'd heard anything untoward but answered Esme telepathically, *Thanks, Esme. Please ask Fen to keep using zer influencer magic to get Fergus to agree.*

Will do, said Esme.

Fergus looked as if he'd like nothing more than to chase them all away, but then Bertram said, "I promise you, Fergus, that Zythrym is correct. And if this doesn't get repaired," continued Bertram, waving his hand around at the destruction, "then the next storm or earthquake could make the land fall into the sea. That isn't in anyone's interests."

"OK," said Fergus reluctantly. "But we are still going to try to topple your government and get our lands back from the dragons."

"That will, of course, depend on the inhabitants of those cities, towns, and villages," said Bertram. "At the moment they don't seem at all interested in what you have to offer. And they were so grateful to become a part of the new joined country of Aerestrea that they gave the dragons lots of help in rebuilding. But let's get your land sorted and repaired first, and then we can talk about other matters."

"I will never live in a land where dragons are treated as equals, rather than mere animals," said Fergus. "My ancestors suffered under the dragons, and we will never forget that."

"Your ancestors were just like you, power hungry and greedy. And they felt threatened by those they didn't understand, including the dragons. Their actions have given us centuries of misunderstandings and problems, one after the other. If you are so against the dragons, and since your current businesses have been pretty well destroyed, you can always restart your businesses in Mlinred or another country where there is no magic and no dragons. But for now, why don't you give us a chance?" said Bertram. "Now, would you like us to begin?"

Everyone looked out over the landscape in front of them. There was a very wide river of mud and debris, containing the remains of trees, buildings, and heaven knows what else, that looked as if it had just flowed across the plain. It was hard to remember that before all the rain, mudslides, and earthquakes, this had been a small, quiet community on the outskirts of the capital. Raymond tried to visualize what could be done, even as Gundryd said privately to him, *Without the land's help, there's not a lot we can do, and we aren't going to get the land's help without a change in attitude from Fergus.*

I know, answered Raymond.

Sapphire said, "Why don't we begin by picking a spot to pile all the debris, somewhere away from whatever rebuilding you want done, Fergus?"

Fergus looked surprised that Sapphire had addressed him, especially after what he'd just said. Zythrym looked over at Fergus and said, "It's mostly your land, Fergus. You will have to make the decisions about what you want here. Are you going to keep it as cheap housing for your workers, or do you have other ideas?"

"I can't imagine that anyone who could afford to live somewhere else would want to stay here," said Fergus.

"Where are those who were living here now located?" asked Bertram.

Fergus just shrugged and said, "I haven't any idea. That's their worry."

Sage said, "Fergus has never looked after his workers. Most of those living here got trapped in his web of forcing them to rent from him and then making sure they never got out of their debts to him."

"You never have understood about good business practices," said Fergus with a snarl.

Malcolm, who'd been looking over the devastation with his own memories of what happened to him and his family, looked up at this statement from

Fergus. After a few moments, he took a deep breath, and then spoke, "It's you who has never understood, Fergus."

Fergus whipped around to look at him and said, "How can you talk? You have nothing now."

"Not true," said Malcolm. "I have my family safe and sound. And I now have a good job, managing various accounts for some of your former friends. I'm free, I am buying a new home in the capital, and I don't owe anyone anything. I'm also looking at all the changes King Bertram has made, and I'm finding that Humphrey and Timothy were correct in what they said at the council meeting. When people are treated decently, paid a living wage, and given a chance, they work even harder."

"Aw, isn't that sweet?" said Fergus in a voice laden with sarcasm.

Malcolm shook his head and said, "You will never get it. As far as what to do with this land, I'm not sure you'll have enough workers to warrant building new housing. Bertram, didn't you say that most of the workers from here had come into the capital and asked for assistance and new jobs?"

The king looked at Fergus and smiled as he said, "Yes, Elicia and her committee are hard at work relocating them. They've all said that they won't come back to working for you."

"Fine," said Fergus. "I can always replace them."

Sapphire tried to get them back on topic. "So if you're not going to build more housing, what do you want to do with this land, and where should we pile the debris?"

Fergus looked around at all the devastation and said, after a long pause, "I don't know. Put the debris over there," he said, pointing to a spot on the very edge of the cliff, "so that if we have more rain, it will just wash into the sea. Once things have been cleaned up so I can see what's here, then I'll figure out what to do with the land."

"OK," said Sapphire. Then she looked at all the dragons and said, "You heard him. Let's pile the debris where he wants it, and then we can see what the possibilities are."

It was a dirty, labor-intensive job, but everyone pitched in. The dragons carted off the biggest of the debris, the remnants of buildings, roofing, walls, and so forth. Ty organized a crew to help dig through the mud and muck for smaller items. It was sad to see pieces of broken furniture buried under several feet of mud.

Esme said, "So many lives turned upside down. Did anyone die in the landslides?"

Elicia said, "There were a number of injuries, mostly broken bones, but thankfully no one was killed."

Gundryd said, "The land made sure of that."

Elicia and Esme looked at him and Esme, "Is that true?"

"Yes," said Gundryd. "The land knows who is responsible and who isn't. Look at what happened with Malcolm and his family. If the land hurts anyone, it will be the likes of Fergus and Zythrym. And the land told me that the families living here were given warning, and that they were also encouraged to go into the capital."

Esme looked at the yellow dragon and said, "You know, we have had reports of people with premonitions of disaster and dreams of a new life in the capital."

Gundryd smiled and said, "The land will never hurt the innocent."

Raymond looked fondly at Gundryd before saying, "I'm so glad that you are in touch with the land. What would she like to see happen here? Do you know?"

Gundryd smiled at Raymond's use of the female pronoun, as the land herself felt that she was mother to all. Then he said, "Actually, I don't know for sure, but I suspect that she would like it if this all fell into King Bertram's control."

Raymond nodded and said, "He would make it a good spot for any who wanted to live here."

They got back to work. Fen joined them after a bit, looking very tired and muddy. "I know we're doing this," ze began, "to try to get Fergus to see that the dragons are good creatures and an asset to any kingdom, but do you think this is going to change anything?"

"How're you doing with your influencer magic?" asked Elicia.

"Not any luck," said Fen. "Fergus had his mind closed to any thought that anything other than a human being has any intelligence at all."

Esme joined them and said, "Actually, I may have an idea."

145

Everyone turned to look at her, and she continued. "I've been looking at Zythrym, and he's definitely planning something. I can't read him entirely, but he doesn't care for Fergus. He thinks the man is stupid and not an asset. He's just about done with using him. Apparently he sees Fergus as a tool to further his goals but now feels that Fergus has reached the end of any usefulness."

"Interesting," said Fen. "Can you think of a way to get Zythrym to dump Fergus? Would that cause Fergus to rethink his alliance?"

"I'm not sure," said Esme. "Have you tried to use your influence on Zythrym?"

"There's something strange about Zythrym," said Fen. "He doesn't ring true on any level."

Chauncey came over to them and said, *You should talk with Fryzal and Illyra. Althea warned us about Zythrym, but she said she couldn't tell us everything—just that he was exceptionally powerful and dangerous.*

"What?" exclaimed Gundryd. "Why didn't I know this?"

Because Althea only dream walks with the three of us, and we just learned this last night. Also, she didn't give us a name, just that someone from her time period was here and was the real villain. Illyra was already suspicious about Zythrym after the council meeting and now, after listening to this morning's discussion, we're sure that Zythrym is the real power. This is the first chance we've had to tell anyone, answered Chauncey.

"Oh," said Gundryd. "I guess that makes sense."

Raymond smiled and said, "We'd better get back to work."

In spite of some minor groans, everyone agreed, and they all returned to the thankless tasks. Raymond said, "This wasn't as hard when we rebuilt the Aerie, because we knew our work was appreciated. But this just seems like we're not making any difference in the way we wanted."

Everyone agreed. After another few hours, King Bertram called a halt for lunch. "Martha and Naomi have been hard at work to provide us with food, which Oscar and Foster have just brought all the way from Dragonwind. There's plenty for all of us, so let's take a well-deserved break."

"Three cheers for Martha and Naomi," someone shouted, and there was a rousing round of cheers as everyone tucked into lunch. Illyra and Fryzal sat with Raymond and Gundryd, as well as Jasper and Bergamen, which gave them a chance to catch up on the latest from Althea.

Bergamen said, "I get the not being able to share too much, as my mother, Windsong, had the ability to foresee things, and she couldn't say a lot of what she knew for fear of changing the future in ways that wouldn't be good. But I suspect it must have been frustrating for her, and I'm sure it is for Althea also."

"Bergamen, I've heard that you have the same gift," said Gundryd.

"No," answered Bergamen, "I have the gift of premonition, and I usually get warnings just seconds before an event happens, so I'm not likely to change anyone's future."

"Just save lives," said Raymond, whose parents and brother had been saved by Bergamen's warning.

Jasper said, "Bergamen's been the hero on several occasions."

Bergamen just blushed, and the conversation moved on.

Once lunch was over, everyone went back to work.

King Bertram, Sapphire, Sage, and Queen Elicia surveyed the work. Sapphire finally said, "What do you think? Can this area be salvaged for anything worthwhile?"

"By Fergus," said Sage, "I'd guess not. But by you and the king, it could become much-needed housing."

"I agree," said Elicia. "We do need more housing, but Fergus will never build affordable housing for those in need. And I heard Gundryd saying that the land wouldn't be helping here the way it did in the Aerie, which means that this is never going to be used properly."

As they were discussing this, they heard Bergamen yell, "Down, everyone."

There was an immediate dive for the ground from everyone who knew Bergamen. Suddenly there was a flurry of arrows flying. One went right over King Bertram, and another over Raymond. Other potential targets included Gundryd and Star, who immediately took flight. Nevertheless, one arrow did find its target. Sage was hit in the right shoulder. She hadn't ducked, as she had never been trained to duck when Bergamen shouted a warning. Elicia had tried to grab her friend but managed only to shift her slightly. However, thankfully, that was enough to save her life.

As she sought to collect herself, Elicia could not help but recall the similar attack that had befallen her, likewise out of nowhere, during a meeting to discuss the rebuilding of the slum district. She shuddered at the thought of the ongoing presence of those who wanted to thwart social progress and community organizing; it seemed such conflicts of wills would remain a fact of Estrean life.

The dragons, who'd all flown out of reach, now chased the shooters, nabbing them in their claws and bringing them to stand before the king. Ty went immediately to Sage and began working on her, pulling the arrow out, bandaging her, and finally using his healing magic.

The bowmen stood in front of the king as he asked, "Who hired you?"

Esme was right next to Bertram so she could look into the minds of the villains. They said nothing, but Esme looked at Bertram and said, "Fergus hired them. He wanted his wife killed. He felt humiliated when she divorced him, and he thinks she and Illyra are responsible for everything that has befallen him."

Just then there was a loud wail and frantic barking. Chauncey and Fryzal came racing up to the king. "Illyra's been kidnapped."

Raymond was right behind them, huffing from having run so fast, and confirmed the worst. "While the arrows were flying, we all ducked down. I made sure Illyra and Fryzal knew the drill. Then we watched the dragons going after these villains," he said, pointing at the men in front of his father. "And that's when Illyra just disappeared. We were so distracted by all the commotion, and we wondered who had been hit when we heard Sage's cry. I was just going to offer to take Illyra to see her mom when I heard Fryzal's shout, and Chauncey started barking like mad."

Fryzal said, "It was Zythrym. He came up behind me and then grabbed Illyra. And you won't believe me, I know, but he just disappeared with her. One minute he had a hold of her, and then in a blink they were gone. Oh, I've failed her."

Sapphire said, "Hold on, Fryzal. You say they just vanished in front of you?"

"Yes," said Fryzal as tears ran down her face.

"How is that possible?" asked Bertram.

"He has magic," said Sapphire. "At a guess, I'd say he can teleport, and not just himself, but a prisoner as well."

"I should have been able to protect her," said Fryzal. "Althea warned us."

Me too, said Chauncey. *Althea warned us that Zythrym was powerful and dangerous, but he still got her.*

"All right, you two," said Sapphire, "You aren't to blame. And we will get Illyra back. Now tell me exactly what Althea told you."

They did, noting that Althea had said something about there being someone else who had a link to the past the way she did. They also mentioned the fact that Illyra was supposed to have really strong magic and that both Fryzal and Chauncey had extra gifts as well. They had not suspected that the one with the link to the past was Zythrym until they noticed how he seemed to be controlling Fergus, and that was now confirmed when they saw him grab Illyra and then vanish.

"OK," said Sapphire. "Show us where all this happened."

Raymond led the way to the spot where they had all been sitting. As he did so, he explained that Illyra didn't know how to react to Bergamen's warnings quickly, so he'd all but pushed her down flat. Only one arrow came even close to them, and that was one he thought had been aimed at him. Once the arrows stopped, well, they thought they were safe and started wondering if anyone had been hurt.

He went on to explain how the situation changed in an instant as Illyra just blinked

out of existence. "I've never seen anything like it. Here's where we were," he concluded as they arrived at the spot where the group had been sitting.

Chauncey immediately started sniffing at the ground. After a few minutes, he said, *Zythrym was here. I'd done what Althea told me, and I'd made sure I could recognize everyone's scent, but especially Fergus and Zythrym because they were against us.*

Chauncey walked a bit away from the spot and said, *Zythrym approached from this direction and came right up behind the spot where Illyra was sitting. But there's no sign of his leaving. According to his trail, he should still be here.*

Sapphire said, "That's what I thought. He walked here, but then he teleported the two of them away, so he'd leave no trail."

Then how am I supposed to track him? moaned Chauncey.

"We have to be smart," said Sapphire. "We have to be able to figure out where he's gone. Let's start by questioning Fergus with Esme's help."

They walked back to where the attack on Sage had taken place. Star was sitting right next to her as Ty finished up bandaging her and then sending his healing magic into her. Oscar and Foster were guarding the shooters as well as Fergus.

Sapphire, after nodding to Esme to assist her, said, "Fergus, where is Zythrym?"

"How should I know?" asked Fergus.

Esme looked at him and said, "So where is his tower?"

Fergus looked stunned by this question. "How do you know about his tower?"

"I know what you know," said Esme. "And I also know that he's left you to take all the punishment. He's abandoned you."

"He wouldn't do that," said Fergus.

"Really?" said Esme sarcastically. "He's done with you. He thinks you're worthless and that you are no longer of any use to him. Do you see him anywhere around here? You're on your own, so I suggest you start talking."

King Bertram said, "You could spend a very long time in my dungeons."

"No," said Fergus. "You wouldn't."

"You tried to kill me, my son, and your former wife, and your so-called friend has now kidnapped a young lady who was under my protection. Why wouldn't I throw you into my dungeons and forget the key?" asked Bertram.

Fergus looked worried now. Esme said, "He's beginning to believe that he has been left to take all the blame."

Fergus jerked up and looked at Esme. "How can you read my mind?"

"Actually, it's not very hard. Just looking at your face gives away most of it. Now where has Zythrym gone?"

"He has a fortress, a really tall tower up in those mountains," said Fergus, pointing north at the mountains behind them.

"He has a place where the landslides originated?" asked Bertram.

Fergus nodded and finally said, "He was pretty proud of it, because he said it was impervious to rain, that it couldn't be destroyed by mudslides since it was firmly fastened into the rock below it by magic—and no, I don't know how—and that earthquakes wouldn't bother it either."

"Can you lead us to it?" asked Sapphire.

"Not now," said Fergus. "I've been there, but that was before all the landslides and so on. They took out the roads to his place. I thought he might have been worried about that, but he said it didn't matter because he didn't use the roads. I didn't understand that at all."

"So he's been teleporting in and out," said Sapphire.

"I don't know anything about any magic," said Fergus. "Now I've told you all I know. Can I leave?"

"Oh, no," said Bertram. "Not until you answer for these thugs you've hired to try to kill several of us."

"But you said..." spluttered Fergus.

"I'll take your cooperation into account when it comes to sentencing you," said Bertram. Then he looked at Oscar and Foster and said, "Can I leave it to you two to transport all these criminals to the dungeon, including Fergus?"

"Of course," said Oscar.

"Our pleasure," said Foster.

"I can help," said Criseda.

Once they were taken care of, King Bertram said, "Now how do we proceed?"

CHAPTER 17

A RESCUE PLAN

Sapphire said, "Althea prepared for this. I think the first thing we need to do is to help Fryzal learn about teleportation."

Ty said, "And I think we all need to relocate to Dragonwind. Obviously we don't need to continue with this clean-up progress. And if we're correct in our guesses about where Zythrym has taken Illyra, his tower is going to be located up in those mountains," he said, pointing to the north, "which may be closer to Dragonwind than it is to here. At least it's no farther."

"That's true," said Sapphire, "and didn't Althea say that somehow another entity, one with evil intent, has come from the same time period that she has? I'm guessing that this must be Zythrym. We definitely need to do some research on him, and that means that we need Driselda and Aloysius."

King Bertram said, "I think we should all relocate to Dragonwind, and that Star and Sage should come as well as Malcolm and his family. We need everyone who has been caught up in this plot of Fergus's to stay together where we can protect each other—especially now that we know that his plot has actually been orchestrated by a much stronger foe."

"Good point," said Sapphire. "Let's relocate and regroup in Dragonwind."

With that decided, the group packed up their things and arranged for their transfer back to Dragonwind. Oscar and Foster, who had just returned after delivering the prisoners to the palace guard, offered to fly back to the capital to pick up Miranda, Molly, and Bertram's kids who were still in the palace.

▲

By midafternoon, everyone was resettled in Dragonwind. The town hall was once again turned into accommodations for visiting guests, and Sage was resting there after being tended to by Ty, Martha, and Blossom. Sapphire asked her and Star if they knew anything more from Althea.

"I don't think so," answered Sage. "She never told me most of what she's now told Illyra, Chauncey, and Fryzal. I suspect that she knows I would never allow Illyra to do anything that would put her in danger. And now she's been kidnapped."

Driselda, who'd brought several boxes of ancient scrolls with her, said, "Did she ever mention Zythrym?"

"No," said Sapphire.

I could fly into the mountains and try to find his tower, said Star.

"No," said Sage. "I don't want you in danger."

Ty said, "I have another idea. Why don't we ask Rupert and Samantha to find spies for us? We've used them before, and most people don't think anything of seeing foxes or squirrels around."

Esme answered, "They have already offered. I told them to be careful, but to search the mountains between here and this morning's clean-up spot."

"Thanks, Esme," said Ty. "Now Driselda, I know you keep an eye on all the descendants of the original riders. Do you know anything about this Zythrym?"

Driselda picked up one of the scrolls from her box and unrolled it. Then she said, "I have the list here of the original riders, and I've found listings for both Althea and someone named Zythrym, as well as Obadiah and all the others. I'd already been working with it to discover where your family, Bertram, came from. And I've verified that Sage and Illyra come from Althea's line.

"As you know, I generally don't follow everyone with the potential for magic because it can easily skip generations, even several generations. I hadn't traced Ty's lineage, for instance, until he asked me to. He's the first in three or four generations to have magic. Normally I wait until there is some kind of abuse of magic, as was the case with Esme's family or Jasper's, before I step in."

"That makes sense," said Bertram. "So you'd had no reason to look into this Zythrym before now?"

Driselda nodded and said, "That's right. I added to the documents so that they were complete but then moved on to others. However, it is interesting to note that there has been someone named Zythrym in each and every generation of that family."

Sapphire said, "Is it just a family name then?"

"We don't know," said Driselda, looking at Aloysius, who also shook his head. "But we did find a troubling reference to the first Zythrym. He was a bonded rider, but he was finally expelled from the Aerie."

"What?" exclaimed Sapphire.

"Yes," said Driselda. "Apparently he wanted to take over the Aerie, but his own dragon told the leader at the time that Zythrym was unstable and wasn't fit to be a rider. Zythrym not only wanted to take over the Aerie, but he also wanted to work with the barons to depose the man who was king of Estrea at the time and make himself the king. It seems that while he initially thought having his own dragon would be the way to power, he soon discovered that the dragons were not at all interested in ruling and never had been. They wanted a cooperation among all living creatures in Estrea, where they could all work together for the good of the entire country. Since this was the opposite of what Zythrym wanted, he decided to kill off the dragons and their riders, joining forces with the barons, so he could take over the country."

There was a stunned silence around the room. Finally, Aloysius said, "It was the only instance in all the histories that Driselda and I have gone through again, very carefully, where a bond was severed, not by the death of one of the pair, but by the nonhuman refusing to remain bonded to the human. Zythrym's dragon, who was called Spruce, was devastated by the actions of his rider, and after reporting those actions to the leader of the time, he just faded away, never to be mentioned in the histories again."

The room was absolutely silent, and those who had bonded partners looked horrified at this news. Finally, Criseda said, "I can't even imagine how Spruce must have felt. The bond in a pairing is so intimate and strong, probably the strongest type of bond of any kind, stronger than lovers or parent-child, or anything else. What had Zythrym done to force Spruce to take such a step?"

"All we can find from the written accounts is that Zythrym had been plotting to take over the Aerie, and he'd done that in part by killing either the dragon or the rider of pairs that opposed him."

"But that's beyond cruel," said Sapphire. "A bonded pair is so close that the loss of one of them usually means the death of the other. That was one reason why the forming of bonds became rarer and rarer over the centuries—because it is an absolute lifetime commitment. It would have been kinder to kill both the dragon and the rider. The fact that he chose to kill only one of the pair is unspeakably cruel."

Driselda nodded and added, "We think that's why Spruce reported his rider. And ultimately, he didn't live long after Zythrym was exiled from the Aerie. Apparently, Althea was instrumental in the exile, as Zythrym had tried unsuccessfully to force her to wed him. When he left, he vowed vengeance on all dragons and their riders, but especially on Althea and any descendants she might have."

"Is there any more news of Zythrym?" asked Ty.

"Not really, other than the fact that there has always been a Zythrym down through the centuries, but I can't tell if anyone has figured out if it is the same rider or a different one. I found Althea's line, but no mention of her continued existence as a dream walker. And Althea seemed to indicate in what she told you guys," Driselda said, looking at Fryzal and Chauncey, "that what he did was different, more like regenerating himself or taking over younger bodies. Honestly, it's quite terrifying."

"I agree," said Sapphire. "We really need to find Illyra. This information explains why he kidnapped her, and she is now in great danger."

"How are we going to do that?" asked Fryzal.

"Well, first of all," said Sapphire, "we need to figure out how to help you learn to teleport. Since no one now living has that magical gift, that's going to be a challenge. But from what Althea showed you in your last dream walk, you're going to need that power."

And I'm supposed to track her, but how can I do that when we don't have anything to track? said Chauncey.

As the group was pondering that, Stella and Mittens came into the hall. Stella was a seven-year-old orphan, small and thin, with brown hair and eyes, who was being fostered by Agatha and Elfrida. She was bonded to Mittens, who also provided her with sight, since a beating when she was still in the slum area of the capital caused her to go blind.

As she entered the room, she looked around and smiled as she found Ty. Stella and Mittens approached Ty, saying, "We want to help."

"Thanks, Stella," said Ty. "That's really kind of you, but I think this is a bit too dangerous for you."

"Mittens can help," Stella insisted. "We've done a lot of practicing at having her be my eyes even when we aren't together. And I know that Rupert and Samantha have already headed into the mountains. If Mittens goes after them, I'll be able to report what they see because I can see what Mittens sees."

"But how far apart can you two be and still communicate?" asked Ty.

"We've tested it from here to the Aerie, and that still works," said Stella. "And if they have to go farther than that, well, I could follow behind Mittens at that same distance and still be able to report back."

Paul and Wilhelmina came in then. They both looked worried, as it brought back memories for them of Paul's capture four years ago and how he had to learn telepathy quickly to save not only himself but also his friends. And while Paul's capture had resulted in a happy outcome, with his bonding to Wilhelmina and his moving to Dragonwind, they weren't so sure that Illyra's kidnapping would have such a good outcome. After all, Paul had been forced to work for nonmagical humans, and obviously, Zythrym was much more powerful.

Paul said, "We want to help as well. You all know that Wilhelmina is the strongest telepath on the entire planet. When Stella shared what she wants to do, we talked, and we think that if Stella rides with me on Wilhelmina, we'll be able to be a relay station for all of you, anyone with telepathy. Wilhelmina can relay messages all over the planet if needed. She can certainly relay anything in Aerestrea."

Sapphire and Bertram looked at each other, and finally Bertram said, "I'm reluctant to have children get involved. It could be very dangerous."

Sapphire nodded, but then Ty spoke, "I would normally agree with you, but face it, the danger that Althea was talking about is going to affect all of us. If Zythrym is that dangerous, none of us will be safe. Dragons may be his main target. I think we can assume that's why he was tricking Fergus to follow him since Fergus is so fearful of dragons and so convinced that they are only dumb animals. But since we know better, humans, foxes, and squirrels—any being willing to defend dragons—will also be in danger."

I can keep Paul and Stella safe, said Wilhelmina, *and you do need help. I understand that Fryzal is going to have to master teleportation. That will take some time, no matter how talented she no doubt is. And she needs to be able to visualize where she is going to teleport, or she could end up killing herself teleporting into a rock or other hazard.*

Sapphire, Bertram, and Ty looked at each other. Then Esme said, "You're also going to need me, as I am the only one who can get a read on Zythrym to try to figure out what he wants. I know I haven't been very successful so far, but I'm the best hope we have for that. I can ride along with Paul and Stella and help Wilhelmina keep them safe."

"It's beginning to look as if we don't have any good options," said Sapphire.

Jasper spoke up then, saying, "I know I can't teleport, but I do have the power of telekinesis, and those two powers are related, so I'm sure Bergamen and I can help Fryzal."

Sapphire said, "Now that's an idea I can get behind, as we can try that here."

Esme said, "And Wilhelmina can take us out now, after Rupert and Samantha, so that once Fryzal learns her new magic, we'll be able to help her decide where to go."

Chauncey spoke up then. *That just leaves me, and I'm determined not to be left behind. I'll also go with Wilhelmina. I can help track not only Zythrym, when we get a lead on him, but others as well.*

Bertram looked at Sapphire and smiled. "It seems that we don't have much of a choice. They've figured out a good plan for a rescue."

"And you can add Bergamen, Edward, and me," said Fen. "If I can get close enough to Zythrym, I may be able to use my influencer magic to keep him from taking any murderous actions. I certainly need to try. And Bergamen's premonitions magic will warn us of any imminent dangers."

Gundryd and Raymond had been in conference, and finally Raymond spoke. "Since Gundryd is the only one who can understand the land, and since Althea was pretty clear that it was going to take help from the land to rescue Illyra and stop Zythrym, we will need to be a part of the rescue."

Gundryd said, "I think Raymond and I need to help Jasper and Bergamen teach Fryzal, and then accompany them to wherever they decide they need to go."

Neither Sapphire nor Bertram looked very happy at all this, but Driselda spoke up, saying, "What these youngsters have proposed does sound reasonable. Dangerous as well, I know, but we will need to use all the resources we have. Let's see what Wilhelmina and her group can find out first. They can leave now, while Fryzal learns to teleport. Then I'd like to say that maybe Star and Sage can take a nap and hope that maybe Althea will dream walk with them to give us more ideas. At least that is the best plan we have."

Reluctantly, Sapphire and Bertram nodded. As they did so, Naomi and Martha came in with a large hamper and said, "We figured you'd OK this wild plan. They'll need food for their journey, so we've packed this hamper."

And just like that, Wilhelmina, Paul, Esme, Mittens, and Stella were off to follow after Rupert and Samantha.

CHAPTER 18

Hunting

Raymond and Gundryd watched as Jasper and Bergamen began teaching Fryzal. They went out onto the village green so they had some space and so Sage could try to nap in the village hall and try to contact Althea.

Once they were centered on the green, Jasper said, "I learned to use telekinesis by moving tons of snow that my father, Rastan, tried to bury Dragonwind under when he was trying to force me to help him. I didn't know how to do it any more than you know how to teleport. But I felt really guilty about what my father was doing, and I was desperate to help the villagers."

Jasper proceeded to tell them about his father's efforts to become the planet's most powerful mage. He'd realized that Jasper was more powerful than he was, so he wanted Jasper to help him take control of Dragonwind and eventually all of Estrea.

However, Jasper had refused. He'd been so happy when the villagers had taken him in and provided him with a home that he certainly wasn't going to aid his father in his mad scramble for power. Rastan figured out that the best way to convince Jasper to help him was to hurt the village, and since he was a weather mage, he just made it snow, nearly burying the village with storm after storm. The result was Rastan's defeat and Jasper's mastering telekinesis.

"I'm thinking that what worked for me might work for you, since I'm sure you're as desperate or even more desperate to save Illyra as I was to save the villagers. What I did was visualize the snow in a different place and then try to push it with my mind. So why don't you try to visualize yourself standing several feet over there," said Jasper, pointing his arm over to the other side of the green, "and see what happens."

Everyone watched as Fryzal screwed up her face and tried to will herself to be standing in a different spot. Nothing happened at first, but then, all of a sudden, Fryzal seemed to disappear and then reappear in front of Martha's bakery.

Raymond, Gundryd, Jasper, and Bergamen all shrieked with joy and applauded Fryzal's success. They worked all afternoon, and by early evening Fryzal was able to get herself all the way to the Aerie and then back again.

At dinner that night, Sage said, "I'm really proud of you, Fryzal. But I wish I'd had as much success as you have. Althea didn't appear to me at all. I'm sorry."

Fryzal tried not to look too disappointed. Raymond said, "We haven't heard anything back from Wilhelmina yet, but we're thinking that we will in the morning and that then we'll need to head out toward them, so that we can all be in range, anyway, to await further developments."

Bertram didn't look very happy at the prospect of Raymond going out, but he knew that he couldn't protect his son and that they really needed to try something.

Sapphire said, "I'm sure you're right, Raymond, but I think I'm going to ask Oscar and Foster to go with you, just for added protection. Gundryd is too young to carry anyone but you, and Bergamen can carry Jasper but not any others, except maybe Mittens. So having Oscar and Foster will be a big help if you need to get away fast. Fryzal can carry Illyra if you can free her, but not Chauncey."

Raymond looked from Sapphire to his father, and he could see the worry in their faces. And he also knew that they were putting a lot of trust in this group of his. "I appreciate that, Sapphire. And I want you to know that we will be really careful. Also, if we need more help, Wilhelmina or Oscar or Foster will be able to contact you.

▲

Meanwhile, Wilhelmina and her group hurried through the woods, moving south along the mountain toward where they thought Zythrym's tower might be. After a couple of hours, they received a telepathic message from Rupert.

He said, *We can see a tower up ahead. There doesn't seem to be anyone around it, though.*

Wilhelmina answered, *We're nearly there. We also can see the tower. Let's stop, out of sight, and see what we can figure out.*

Sounds like a good plan, said Rupert as he looked up at the tall, skinny, octagonal tower made of stone. There were very few windows, and the ones he could see were very small. The tower looked as if it had just one room on each level, with, he assumed, some kind of interior staircase.

Once Wilhelmina and company caught up to Rupert and Samantha, they looked for a cave where they could hide and plan. It didn't take them long to find a medium-sized cave, and they all moved inside.

Stella said, "So is Zythrym in the tower?"

Rupert shook his head and said, *We haven't heard or seen him. We just don't know. Esme, can you sense anything?*

Esme was very still and quiet for a few minutes before saying, "I'm not sure. But it's getting late, and we are all tired. I suggest we stay here for the night, taking turns on watch, and see what the morning brings."

Wilhelmina said, *That sounds like an excellent plan. I think we should see what Martha and Naomi sent with us. Then after we've eaten, I'll take the first watch so that the rest of you can get some sleep. Chauncey, I'd like you to sleep all night long, in case Althea should want to contact you.*

OK, said Chauncey. *But I wish I could do more.*

I know, said Wilhelmina, *but I think your turn will come. Esme, can you stand watch for a couple hours in the middle of the night? I don't need more sleep than that.*

Esme nodded and said, "Certainly."

"What about Mittens and me?" asked Stella.

Get a good night's sleep, you two. Esme and I have this, said Wilhelmina. *And Rupert and Samantha will assist as well.*

Illyra looked around the room she was imprisoned in. She was all alone, and the room was very tiny, with only a narrow bed and a dresser that had a bowl for washing on the top. There was a window, a very small one, above the bed, but she couldn't see anything outside that she recognized. She'd seen no one since she'd been kidnapped, and she didn't even know how that had happened. The last thing she remembered was ducking for cover with Raymond, Gundryd, Fryzal, and Chauncey as she heard her mother scream and saw arrows flying. And now she was on her own.

She thought back to the night before and her dream walk with Althea. Althea had not told them a lot, but she did say that Illyra, Fryzal, and Chauncey each had special magic. Fryzal's was teleportation, which Illyra thought someone had used to bring her here, wherever here was, so maybe that meant that Fryzal would be in a position to rescue her eventually.

Her own gift, as Althea had reminded her, was telekinesis. She knew that to be true since she'd developed it in her efforts to rescue Fryzal. But how was that supposed to help her now?She looked around the room. She noticed a door on the wall where the dresser was. Suddenly an idea popped into her head. What if she moved the small dresser? Where would she like it? Then she thought that whoever had kidnapped her would eventually show up wanting something. What if she put the dresser in front of the door? Would that keep them out?

The more she thought about it, the more she really wanted that dresser to block the door. She didn't really think that in the grand scheme of things it would make any real difference, but why not try? She concentrated and quickly managed to move the dresser so that it was blocking the door.

However, as soon as that was done, Zythrym appeared in her room, and she realized how silly it was to block a door against someone who could teleport. Zythrym looked at her and said, "Finally. I have the last living person from Althea's lineage. You are not as important to my plans as killing off the dragons, but you should know that you are in danger now only because your ancestor rejected me and caused my original plan to fail."

"Althea has told me all about your misguided and evil attempt to take over Estrea. It won't succeed now any better than it did in the past. You are a miserable excuse for a man—even worse than my father, and that's saying a lot," said Illyra.

Zythrym reached out and slapped her, but Illyra stood her ground. He looked at her with a puzzled look at first. She could almost see the wheels turning in his head. She realized that he'd been expecting her to act terrified or impressed or heaven knows what else. All she felt was disgust at his behavior. She would do whatever she could to stop him.

"You thought you could force Althea to marry you. She wasn't going to be forced, and neither am I. You killed your own bonded mate. I really do feel for Spruce, and I applaud his courage to report you for your evil ambitions. You are the only one who has no courage or honor."

"How dare you say that?" said Zythrym. "I'm much more capable to rule than any of these weaklings. They have no clue how to control and rule a nation."

"There you are so wrong," said Illyra. "Power and force may seem to work for the short term, but keeping people as slaves, as my father and the barons have tried to do, ultimately fails. This nation now has the example of what kindness and fair treatment can do, and we won't go back. You will fail, and I'll do my best to be part of that end for you, just as Althea did centuries ago."

"You're out of the equation now," said Zythrym. "You and your pitiful efforts won't make any difference. You will never leave this room."

With that, he slammed the dresser over to the other side of the room and began to open the door. Illyra reached for the dresser and, using her new-found powers, hurled it at him, knocking him sideways and causing the dresser to hit him hard in the side of the head. Unfortunately, it wasn't enough to knock him out, but a corner of the dresser did gash his forehead.

Zythrym flung out an arm, sending the dresser toward Illyra, who could only jump out of the way. Then Zythrym threw open the door, saying, "You'll regret that action," as he stepped through the door, slamming it after him.

Illyra sat down heavily on her bed. She felt so alone. She couldn't see much from the tiny window, but the little she had seen hadn't given her any hope. Zythrym obviously had an abundance of servants, as she'd seen a number of men going back and forth outside, and she could now hear him shouting at them, telling them that they were not to open the door or give the prisoner any food or drink.

And so far, she hadn't been able to contact Fryzal or Chauncey. *I must be too far away from them*, she thought. She sure hoped they were OK. Ty and Criseda, as well as Sapphire, would look after them, she was positive. And they would be coming for her, she was sure. But Zythrym was so powerful, and from what she'd seen and heard, he had a lot of servants. She didn't want her friends to be hurt in an attempt to rescue her.

Right after Zythrym had captured her, she'd wondered why anyone would want her. She'd had no idea. But now she knew, and what he said had fit with the brief information Althea had given her, so she knew that this was really personal for Zythrym. That made her feel even more alone.

She'd just started making friends. She liked Raymond and thought he was really bright and also fun. And Esme, Jasper, and Fen were also so nice to her. She'd never had real friends. She'd had to take care of her mother, and her father hadn't let her meet anyone her own age. But Dragonwind was such a wonderful place filled with kind people.

She was really looking forward to working on the queen's committee to help those in need. But would she ever get out of here? And was there any way she could do so without endangering her new friends? And could she really help stop Zythrym? The tasks seemed so daunting.

She looked up at the tiny window above the bed, and she realized it was definitely dark outside. She pulled the thin blanket over herself and put her head on the pillow. Sleep overtook her.

Althea came to her then. "Illyra, I'm sorry this has happened to you. Fryzal, Chauncey, are you there?"

"Yes," they each answered. Illyra realized that her friends were in the dream as well. "Where are you?" she asked.

Chauncey answered first. *I'm with Wilhelmina and some others, and we're outside a tall tower where we think you are being held.*

"Really?" said Illyra.

"And I'm in Dragonwind with Raymond, Jasper, and Bergamen. I spent the day learning how to teleport, and we're coming to that tower tomorrow," said Fryzal.

"I miss you both so much," said Illyra.

"Now listen, you three," said Althea. "It's hard to dream walk with all three of you when you are in such different places. But I have information that you absolutely must have.

"First, you will all be in roughly the same place by morning. Raymond, Gundryd, and Fryzal as well as Jasper and Bergamen are flying here now that Fryzal has learned to teleport. You will need everyone to help. I'll let Gundryd fill in the details, but I will say that the land is really upset, and she has been working to undermine this tower. When it falls, you three will be needed to save Illyra.

"Chauncey, you will need to trace her in the rubble. Illyra, you will need to use your telekinesis to give yourself a safe place in the rubble and also, if needed, to keep Zythrym captured. And Fryzal, you will have to teleport Illyra out without letting Zythrym tag along with her. Do you all understand?"

There was silence for a few heartbeats, and then they all said, "Yes."

"I know it seems like a daunting task, but have faith in yourselves and trust each other as well as your friends. You will know if you succeed if I disappear. Zythrym and I are tied together in a way I can't entirely explain, but my task is to help you so that you can collectively defeat Zythrym. When that happens, I will fade away, as will he. And I must warn you all that he must be defeated, even if that means that some of you don't survive. I sincerely hope that won't be the case, but that's just how serious this is."

The three of them were very quiet. Then Fryzal said, "It seems as if the riskiest moment will be when I teleport Illyra out of wherever she is."

"I'm afraid you are correct, Fryzal. It will be very risky, but you will also have extra help, as Gundryd will explain tomorrow. None of you will be alone, and the land is really in charge of all this. Now I have to go. If this all plays out the way I hope it will, I may not get another dream walk with you, but I have faith in you, and I've really enjoyed working with you all."

"Thank you, Althea. It's been wonderful to get to know you," said Illyra.

Sure has, said Chauncey.

"And thanks for all the help," added Fryzal.

Once Althea had left each of them, they heard another voice. *Hi, you three. This is Wilhelmina here, and I wanted you to know that I've been working hard to combat the telepathy block that Zythrym has set up to keep you, Illyra, from receiving communications from anyone. I'm sure that has made you feel extremely lonely.*

But I have sorted that out. I also heard what Althea told you all in her dream walk, and I want to be sure you know that you have a lot of friends who are here to help you. You definitely are not alone anymore. And by morning, all of us will be near each other. So please don't worry, and Illyra, by morning you'll be able to talk with both Fryzal and Chauncey. So sweet dreams. I am the strongest telepath on the planet, and nothing is going to stop us.

Each of the three of them thanked Wilhelmina. Illyra felt slightly less alone, although it was very cold and dark in the tower, and the only blanket on the bed was extremely thin.

Fryzal was worried because she was so far away from Illyra and Chauncey, but she trusted Wilhelmina and was pleased that she'd be able to talk with both Illyra and Chauncey tomorrow. She only hoped that she'd learned enough about teleportation to be able to save Illyra. That was a daunting responsibility.

Chauncey looked up at the tower and wished he could share Illyra's bed, not only to be closer to her but also to give her his warmth. He worried about being able to find her when the tower collapsed, but he was a good rescue dog. He'd just have to trust Wilhelmina.

Finally, each of the three of them fell asleep and slept soundly until morning.

As they slept and Wilhelmina kept watch, she heard a telepathic voice saying, *Help me!*

She answered, *Who are you?*

My name is Thrym, and I'm a prisoner. My father is holding me captive, but I really want to stop him. That young girl he's holding prisoner in the top of this tower doesn't deserve his anger.

How do you know all this?

I can't explain. I just need to get away from him. You don't know what he's capable of.

Wilhelmina thought long and hard. Who could this person be? Was this some kind of trick, or was it a true call for help? Finally she said, *I don't know what I can do at the moment, but I would recommend that you get out of the tower, if that's where you are now.*

And then you'll find me?

We will try.

After that, Thrym said no more, and Wilhelmina was left to wonder what was going on.

CHAPTER 19

THE LAND STEPS IN

The next morning Illyra woke up to the sound of Fryzal's telepathic voice calling to her. She nearly wept with joy. Except for last night's dream with Althea, it had been so long since she had heard from her. She knew it was only a day, but given what she'd been through, it felt like forever.

Illyra, are you there? Wilhelmina said she'd fixed things so we can talk again.

Illyra chuckled and then said, *I'm here. How are you? I hear you can teleport now.*

I'm doing fine now that I can talk to you, and since you can move things with your mind, we'll be quite the pair now.

Illyra liked Fryzal's enthusiasm, but she was still very worried that they wouldn't actually be able to stop Zythrym. *So is everyone here now, and what's the plan?*

Gundryd is working at finding out what the land has done and what she wants us to do. Then he'll tell us. I do know that the land has been working hard to bring Zythrym down.

OK, said Illyra. *I sure hope there's a good plan.*

They all waited as Gundryd conferred with the land. Finally, he called everyone together. Everyone else was in one spot. Only Illyra was in the tower away from the others, but Gundryd spoke telepathically so that Illyra wouldn't feel left out.

The land has been working on capturing Zythrym for some time. This tower is built on a pillar of bedrock that is several hundred feet down, and the land can cause an earthquake at its base. But there needs to be some place for the tower to go once the base is broken. In the last few weeks, the land has been excavating a chasm below the tower, and that chasm is now several thousand feet deep. When the pillar of bedrock collapses, the tower should just drop down into the chasm.

At the moment, Zythrym is being distracted by Star and the dragons flying over and around the tower. He's staying at the base of the tower, trying to shoot them. He has lots of men who are also firing arrows. As we all know, Illyra is at the top of the tower. So if the tower drops vertically, Zythrym will end up several thousand feet down inside the chasm. Illyra will be far closer to the surface, although she'll still be maybe a thousand feet deep.

Once the tower collapses, Illyra, you will need to find a way to move upward, while at the same time watching to be sure that Zythrym doesn't follow you. Chauncey, you will have to find Illyra, or the point on the surface that is closest to her. Fryzal, you will then go to the spot Chauncey finds and teleport Illyra out, being very sure that Zythrym doesn't latch on to her and follow her.

As soon as Illyra is free, the dragons and Wilhelmina will start burying the tower in all the dirt that the land has excavated to make the chasm. That tower must be buried quickly and deeply. So that's the plan. We need to carry it out now.

There are so many ways, said Fryzal, *that this could go horribly wrong.*

Wilhelmina said, *We have to try. Let's stay positive and be ready to roll with any needed changes. Gundryd, I think you need to tell the land that we're ready. Delaying will only make us worry more. Illyra, get ready for the destruction of the tower.*

▲

Illyra decided the best place for her would be sitting down, so she sat on the edge of the small bed. She'd barely gotten comfortable when the tower began to shift back and forth. She braced herself by putting her hands on each side of her so she remained steady.

It didn't take long before it felt as if the bottom was dropping out of her stomach as the entire tower began to descend very rapidly. The tower also seemed to tip back and forth vertically. The bottom was going down, down a long way, as the top sort of swayed.

Then she heard an earth-shattering shriek. It didn't take her long to figure out that the shriek, a loud shout of "No," had to be Zythrym. After all, he was in the base of the tower and thus was plummeting rapidly, at least a thousand feet downward, she thought. As the top of the tower collapsed, the ceiling of her room cracked, and debris rained down on her.

Quickly she put her hands up and used her telekinesis magic to deflect the falling debris. Then she decided also to move the ceiling off to the side of the tower so that she could see what was above her. She felt less claustrophobic when she could see the sky above, even though the sky was getting farther and farther away as she descended. The sky was bright, but her room was getting hotter and hotter. She was glad she could see some sky, but that view soon became smaller and less comforting as the tower continued its descent.

She could see dragons flying overhead, and it looked as if they were each carrying rocks, which they dropped into the chasm as the tower descended. She assumed that was being done to discourage Zythrym from trying to teleport out of the chasm. They had to keep him trapped.

In fact, what Illyra couldn't see was that there was a battle raging outside the tower. Sapphire directed the dragons to fly close to the tower, shooting fire near the archers who were firing on Zythrym's command. She'd commanded the dragons not to kill any of the men but to burn all their arrows. As she flew overhead, she could see the men trying to follow Zythrym's orders. There were a lot of men, but the dragons had no trouble stopping all their arrows.

She heard Zythrym shout, "Kill those dragons, you fools."

One of his men shouted back, "Just how are we to do that? The dragons are burning all our arrows before they can find a target."

"I don't care how," said Zythrym. "Just do it."

His soldiers renewed their efforts as the dragons soared and dived around them, totally distracting everyone from anything else and ensuring that Zythrym stayed at the bottom of the tower to direct the action. It was obvious that the dragons were all but enjoying the encounter, and that they were very effective at keeping Zythrym just inside the bottom of the tower, dropping rocks right in front of his door whenever he stuck his head out.

Finally, there was a bone-jarring crash as the tower hit the bottom of the chasm. This crash caused the tower to break apart, and Illyra was thrown off to the side, hitting the wall of the chasm hard and breaking her right arm. Then a lot of debris and rocks threatened to bury her, but she used her left arm and her telekinetic abilities to protect herself. When the debris finished falling, she found that she'd been able to create an arch over her, which looked stable. She cried out, "Anyone there?" and then was silent, listening.

She heard Zythrym wail, "My leg," and hoped that meant he'd also been injured.

Chauncey called to her. *Are you OK?*

Illyra said, *Sort of. I think my right arm is broken, but otherwise I'm OK. Can you see me? I'm under an arch.*

She then heard Fryzal say, *Chauncey, have you found her?*

Chauncey said, *Yes, she's down here, under that pile of rocks, I think. I can't see her, but she says she's under an arch.*

Fryzal looked down into the chasm and saw where Chauncey meant. She reached out telepathically to Illyra, saying, *Can you move anything to indicate where you are?*

Suddenly a small rock flew up from next to the arch that Chauncey had indicated. Fryzal shouted, "Got it! Thanks!"

Be careful, said Chauncey. *She said her arm is broken.*

Fryzal nodded and then said to Illyra, *Now that the debris has stopped falling, can you open up the arch safely, so I can see you?*

Illyra called back, *I'll try. Hang on.*

Just then, Criseda and Ty flew overhead, and Ty shouted out, "We can see Zythrym trying to climb up. And it looks as if he's dragging a young man with him. We need to knock them back down. Don't shift that arch until we have him taken care of."

OK, said Illyra and Fryzal together.

Oscar and Foster joined Criseda and Ty in their efforts to halt Zythrym's attempted escape. They dropped giant rocks right next to where the tower was sitting in ruins, and one of the rocks caught Zythrym on the head, knocking him out as both he and whomever he was holding were thrown back down into the chasm.

"You got him," said Raymond, who was riding Gundryd above the chasm so they could keep watch for the land.

"Nice shot, Foster," said Ty. "Now Fryzal, see if we can get Illyra out of there and then seal up this chasm."

Fryzal nodded and called again to Illyra, "OK, can you either move or take down the arch so we can see you?"

By now Illyra was in severe pain, but she knew she had to help Fryzal. After all, she'd just learned to teleport, and she needed to be able to see Illyra. Fryzal also knew she was injured and would be worried about hurting her more. So Illyra gritted her teeth, took a deep breath, lifted her left arm, and began to take apart the arch. She'd moved several rocks from the top to the side when Fryzal shouted, "I can see you! That's good. Now hold still."

Everyone was watching Fryzal as she attempted to teleport Illyra, but suddenly Raymond shouted, "Look out."

Gundryd also called out, "Fryzal, no. Not yet. Zythrym is trying to latch onto Illyra."

Sure enough, Zythrym had managed to move in a blink of an eye so that he was right next to Illyra. He also still had the young man gripped in his right hand. Fryzal quickly abandoned her teleportation spell. Instead, she started another, one that only included Zythrym and the other person, and used it to send them to the absolute bottom of the chasm. Then she quickly latched onto Illyra before Zythrym could try again and yanked Illyra out of the chasm.

Illyra let out a cry, and Fryzal raced over to her. "I'm so sorry. I wanted to be gentle, but I had to move fast before Zythrym could do his own teleportation to get back to you. It appears he's weak from being hit with Foster's rock, so he can only teleport a short distance."

Illyra nodded, trying to cradle her arm. Criseda landed next to her so Ty could jump off, and then all the dragons, including Criseda, began filling the chasm. They took special pleasure in aiming rocks and debris at Zythrym. They were also aided by the land herself, who caused vast quantities of dirt and debris to slide into the chasm as the land around the chasm collapsed.

Suddenly there was a torrential downpour, a storm that washed a wide swath of land into the hole. As the flood hit, Raymond and Gundryd flew low over the chasm, and Raymond shouted, "Zythrym is swimming to the south wall, dragging someone with him. Oh, he's disappeared. I can't see him anymore."

Ty said, "Do you suppose he drowned?"

Raymond kept watch, and finally Gundryd said, "He took a real chance. He teleported without any destination in mind, and he could have ended up inside a solid object. But the land tells me that he and whomever he was holding onto were lucky. They've landed at Aerestrea's southwestern border with Mlinred, a country that was mostly agricultural, with no close relationship with Aerestrea, and no magic or dragons. It is about five hours south from the Aerie and maybe two hours south from the capital. He then crawled with the young man into Mlinred."

"What?" said Illyra. "He's still alive?"

Gundryd said, "Apparently. But the danger to the dragons and our land is gone, at least for the moment. We may have to deal with him eventually, but the land assures us we are safe for now. Zythrym has lost everything and barely escaped. He is also injured, with a nasty head wound. It will take him time to regroup and rise again."

Ty looked at Illyra and said, "Let me see that arm, and then I think we should all return to Dragonwind. This has been a harrowing experience for everyone, but especially for you, Illyra, and Chauncey and Fryzal.

Ty used his healing power to move the bone in Illyra's right arm back into place and then he found a branch, which he trimmed and shaped into a splint to bind it. Once he'd made her as comfortable as he could for the moment, he said, "This will help until we get to Dragonwind. Then we can set this properly."

"Thank you," said Illyra.

Ty helped Illyra to get onto Fryzal, and as she and Fryzal flew, Fryzal voiced the concern that Illyra had been feeling. "Did we fail?"

"I don't know," said Illyra. "Gundryd seemed to think that we did something, but I just don't know if it was enough. I don't think this is over yet. I sure wish Althea could tell us more."

"Me, too," said Fryzal. "I don't understand any of this."

▲

Once all those on dragons were back in Dragonwind, Ty ushered Illyra into Martha's kitchen so that her arm could be properly tended. It didn't take him and Martha long to treat the arm, and Illyra was much more comfortable keeping her splinted arm in the sling Martha provided.

Soon Esme, Rupert, Samantha, Chauncey, and Wilhelmina arrived in Dragonwind. As they ate dinner, the discussion turned to the events of the day. Ty said, "Gundryd, can you tell us what happened to Zythrym?"

"I'm sorry, but I don't know a lot," he began. "The land is calm now and seems to think that the immediate crisis has passed, that Zythrym is now in the neighboring land of Mlinred, and that he's considerably weakened. Also, as Sage knows, magic doesn't work in Mlinred because they have no dragons, so that will slow him down as well. None of us is currently in danger, but there is no doubt that Zythrym will be back."

"That's not very comforting," said Raymond. "And who was that person who teleported with him?"

Wilhelmina said *I may have an idea about that. Last night I received a call for help from a young man named Thrym. He said his father was holding him prisoner.*

"What?" said Ty.

I didn't know if it was a real call for help or just a trap, but we couldn't do anything then anyway. All I could do was tell him to try to get out of the tower. I guess he didn't succeed in that.

Esme said, "I know I wasn't a lot of help today, but when Zythrym nearly latched onto Illyra just as Fryzal was getting ready to teleport her, I was able to read great joy in him and a sense that he'd now be able to take out the dragons. However, that thought only lasted a second or two. Next he and I guess this Thrym were tumbling back into the chasm with thoughts of wondering how he could have been defeated. I think he's suffered a substantial setback, but I agree; he's not defeated, and he's not giving up."

Ty said, "Well, that's enough for tonight. I think we all need some sleep. Tomorrow I'll talk with King Bertram and find out what he and Sapphire have planned for Fergus and the others he arrested today."

Illyra, Chauncey, Fryzal, and Blossom headed back to Blossom's cave, and soon Illyra, Chauncey, and Fryzal were asleep.

As they slept, Althea came to them. Before she spoke, she looked fondly at the trio. Then she said, "You three did far more than I thought you'd be able to."

"We did?" said Illyra. "But Zythrym got away."

"I know," said Althea. "But he's much, much weaker. And he's in a land that doesn't have magic. I know you and your mother came from Mlinred, Illyra, but your mother's magic didn't work there. That was a good thing, as Fergus had no idea what powers his new bride had. However, it also meant I couldn't protect her there. Then, when they moved here and you were born, I was able to dream walk with her and let her know what she needed to do to protect both herself and you.

"But what that means for us now is that while Zythrym is still a hateful, driven man, determined to annihilate dragons, he's no more powerful in Mlinred than any other person. And he's also very weak and injured after his time in the tower collapse. That will give you three, as well as Gundryd, time to mature and strengthen your powers before you have to face him again.

"Honestly, I didn't expect you all to survive yesterday's encounter, but we had to try. The stakes were too high. But the fact that I'm still here and everyone is safe at the moment means that I have time to teach you three, and we have time to be together, and for that I'm extremely grateful."

So are we, said Chauncey.

Next in the Dragonwind Series:
Dragons, Dreamers, and the Land

About the Author

Daphne Ashling Purpus has a great love of fantasy literature, cultivated during her career as a librarian and teacher. She now lives and writes on beautiful Vashon Island in the Pacific Northwest, where she tutors students of all ages at the local alternative schools, StudentLink and FamilyLink.

A prolific fiction writer, Purpus is the author of fourteen fantasy novels about dragons, including *Dragon Rider; The Egg That Wouldn't Hatch; Dragon Magic; The Dragon Who Chooses Twice; The Girl, the Gryphon, and the Dragon; The Mage's Dilemma; The Seer's Challenge; The Dragon and the Unicorn; The Fox, the Stag, and the Dragon; Dragon Sanctuary; Dragons, Mages, and Magic; Dragons and Other Outliers; Dragons, Waifs, and Influencers;* and most recently, *Dragons in Peril.* Her poetry is published in *A Year of Haiku.*

In addition to tutoring, writing, and reading, Purpus can be found caring for her dog and three cats.

www.ingramcontent.com/pod-product-compliance
Lightning Source LLC
Chambersburg PA
CBHW060152130626
46556CB00006B/2604